American BeheMouth

By

Jason Covington

Dedication

To my fellow fishers in life, who have fished, loved, and lost.

It is better to have fished and lost than never to have fished at all.

Quote borrowed from Alfred, Lord Tennyson's *In Memoriam*,

Canto XXVII, 1850:

"'Tis better to have loved and lost than never to have loved at all."

Table of Contents

World-Record Castaic Bass 5

Lake of the Ozarks' State-Record Bass 17

Crab Orchard Lake, Illinois 24

The Science of Growing Giant Bass 31

A Generational Fishing Legacy 37

Building My Bass Lake..60

A Weekend at the Lake 74

Lake Fork..85

The Shock of a Lifetime 99

A Fishy Dreamlike State 112

End of the Summer Dream..122

A New World-Record* Bass...136

Back to Reality 144

Epilogue 156

About the Author 158

About "American BeheMouth" 159

Chapter 1

World-Record Castaic Bass

The giant Castaic bass went for a short run to the side of the boat, but I steered her back under the middle. My fishing partner stood ready with the net over the side. One quick rush, maybe too eagerly, but luckily, he scooped up the fish!

This was merely another day on Castaic Lake in Southern California in 1992. I wasn't a pro who fished the lake every day. In fact, I had only recently heard about the record-sized bass caught in Castaic. I had been fishing for bass all my life, starting at the age of four with a stick, line, and hook. When I was six, my grandfather formally schooled me with a fly rod and popper on my aunt's lake in Southern Illinois.

I had always dreamed of catching a world-record bass. After moving to California when I was 10, my friend Glen and I would ride our bikes to the nearest reservoir, Vasona, for our own big bass contest. We raced there with casting gear and tackle boxes strapped to the backs of our bikes. As I rode my bike down the path along the lake, I saw a fish swirl, so I paused right there to cast, with my bike still between my legs. The championship was mine as I reeled in the big bass of the tournament, yelling at Glen, "Hey, take my bike! I have a big one!"

"No way," he said as he rode past. "What do you think this is—a charity tournament?"

I let the bike fall to the ground, scraping it into the paved path in order to land the bass. Two and a half pounds, the Zebco De-Liar Scale read. Tournament winner: Jay.

Glen wasn't cheering as he handed me his tackle box to pick out the lure of my choice. The hurt: a $5 Rapala Shad Rap—a prize big enough to make a kid jump in the lake after a lost one, even in winter weather.

This trip to Castaic was the manifestation of those childhood dreams. With some time on my hands after graduating from college, I was still struggling with the question of how I was going to support myself through life. After only a few phone calls, I learned of a guy who had been a local Castaic tournament winner so many times that people cried foul. He had been kicked out of the circuit without even a fair inquiry into the accusations. He had figured out the pattern for winter trophy bass when no one else could. Later I would find out that he was going through a breakup with his wife. His construction job had some setbacks, and he had days off without pay.

I had not been fishing for a long time and was curious to see Castaic. I anticipated some action but never expected the fishing that day to be like the stock market rallies of the time.

During the drive, Brian told me that some heavyweight bass were still on beds. From his years of experience, he knew exactly where to go, and we launched the boat. We put on four-inch worms with 1/16 ounce weights, Texas-rigged. I marveled at the steep slopes of the banks and wondered where spawning flats would be. The sides of the hills were rocky and dry, despite average spring rainfall. We pulled in three or four bass, hooked in front of brush piles from the first flat. They were all two to three pounds but clearly were young fish. They felt like strong fighters on the six-pound line with ultra-light spinning gear.

Another boat idled by, and the fish at our spot spooked. Brian seemed to have a plan on where to go next: the back end of a cove with a flat. The spot was as fishy as could be. He anchored the boat parallel to the end of the cove so I could pitch into the back pocket, a peculiar shady spot with branches hanging over the water. I say "peculiar" because Castaic did not have many trees or shady spots. Most of the shoreline appeared dry and rocky, even in April.

The first cast did not hit the mark, but I fished it in anyway. Nothing. The second cast was perfect. The bank took the impact of my pitch, and the worm bounced gently into the farthest spot. I didn't shake it more than a few times before I felt the bump and set the hook.

The fish didn't have anywhere to go except straight at us. It swam like a torpedo under the boat past us. I reeled as fast as I could to keep up the slack and shoved my rod about four feet under the boat with my body hanging over in perfect timing. Nonetheless, I felt the snap. The limber rod and light line were no match for the sheer weight and strength of the fish, even with the reel's drag set perfectly.

"Do you see what I was telling you?" Brian said.

"Yes," I said, flabbergasted. I talked to Brian for a few minutes in an attempt to understand what had happened. Of course, I always try to figure out what I did wrong and what I could have done differently. This time, though, I was over-analyzing.

Brian calmly interrupted me. "There was nothing you could have done. They like the four-inch worm, but they won't take it on heavy line or with a heavy weight. You won't get bit."

My mathematical mind recalculated. "What about a different set up? I want to land one like that!"

Brian started tinkering in the rod locker. He brought out a seven-foot rod, a casting reel, a jig box, and some pork. "Most people don't throw them here, but for the bigger bass, they should work the same here as everywhere else. You can get away with 10-pound test. The rod can handle a bigger fish, too."

I tied on a black jig and pork trailer, and he motored over to some other main lake spots.

Brian said, "These are some of the deeper spawning spots. They should hold some of the bigger fish. A jig fished slowly enough over one of the beds will trigger some strikes."

We fished for a few hours without any results, and Brian could see my frustration. "You said you wanted a big fish. We're after one fish now, not the numbers we would get with the split shot rigs and four-inch worms."

"Yeah, yeah," I said. "You're right. That's what I'm after."

Right as I said that, Brian slammed the hook into a big bass. I netted it as he pulled it up to the side.

"Six and a half," he said. He didn't need to weigh it. It was a common size for a female fish.

About 20 minutes later, I hooked one and reeled it in. Same size and shape. Brian took a picture of me and the fish, holding a white Poe's Plug next to its jaw.

"That's my secret that landed me in so much trouble," Brian said. "I would always lie about what I caught my fish on in tournaments. Why tell everyone else your secret? If I told everyone my secret to catching suspended fish, I would no longer have an edge. That would be dumb."

"After two times with a 50-pound stringer and saying I caught them on a Poe's Plug, everyone knew I was lying, at least about what I was using. But why should I have to tell the whole league what I was using? I came up with the idea on my own."

"What was it?"

Brian gave me a look of surprise. "I'm not telling. I spent two years figuring it out. I can catch suspended bass in the winter when nobody else can."

"A vertical jig?"

"No."

"A grub?"

"No."

I listed off about 10 other ideas.

"No. You're not going to figure it out." He continued fishing.

I focused back on fishing. The sun was high in the sky. Our chances for a big fish were probably over. Another boat idled by, and they yelled, asking how we did.

"A few up to six and a half," Brian said. "Split shot rigs."

"One eight," a guy yelled back. "Split shot."

With them motoring past and us out-fished, I counted the day as over and started to pack up.

Brian did not pay me any attention. He motored over to a point that juts out into the main lake. "Right there," he pointed to a spot about 30 feet off the end of the point.

I made a long cast and let the jig sink in free spool for about 35 to 40 seconds. I hopped it gingerly a few times and felt it go lifeless. A fish had picked it up and was swimming toward me. I set the hook hard as I reeled in the slack. Luckily, Brian had turned down the drag enough to compensate for my eagerness to hook—as if we were in Florida with 20-pound test line among water lilies.

The fish was a brute, and I held the rod high and let her play out. She stayed in deep water, swimming back and forth. No antics under the boat, and no brush piles nearby.

Brian was calm and didn't say anything at first. He readied the net. Only then did he tell me, "Start pumping her in."

I lifted up the rod and reeled down the slack, slowly and gently about 10 times before we could see the fish about 15 feet down. "Oh my God," Brian said.

The fish pulled out the drag for a short run. Then I continued directing her toward the net.

"Holy crap," Brian said. I knew the fish was enormous when he said that. I was feeling a little shaky. "Just a couple more," he said.

The fish went for a short run to the side, but I steered her back to the middle of the boat where Brian stood ready with his body over the side with the net.

One quick rush, maybe too eager, and Brian had it. Before he could even lift the fish, which barely fit in the net, the bass rammed its head against the net and came alive in a frantic frenzy. The sheer strength of it about pulled the net out of Brian's hand, throwing off his center of gravity. This allowed the rim of the net to turn to the side enough for the world-record bass to break the 10-pound test line like a one-pound tippet.

"Oh my God, I'm gonna be sick!" Brian screamed across the lake.

I was shaking so hard that I still hadn't said anything. Finally I mustered a "How big was she?"

"A world record—that's what. Twenty-five and some change, easy."

Needless to say, that ended the trip. Brian was depressed. I was content to have caught something, never expecting to have hooked a world record on my first trip to Castaic. How could that be possible?

We fished together only once more a few months later. The weather was too hot, and we only caught fish to three pounds. He could not eat or sleep, devastated by his divorce. He was clearly torn up as much about loss in his personal life as he was about the loss of the fish. How many worthy men like Brian have pursued this quest into oblivion with nothing to vouch for it? I never heard from Brian again, and his phone number was disconnected. This close call with the world record bass charged me up to go after it with everything I had; the pursuit was

intoxicating and addictive.

When my grandfather was my age, he built power lines

across the Rockies by hand. I reasoned if I were to step up to a

life's challenge, I could catch this fish.

Chapter 2

Lake of the Ozarks' State-Record Bass

I was on my way to Illinois in the fall of 1992 as a graduate student when I first had the chance to fish in Missouri. The day was significant as my first experience in Missouri, where I would eventually settle.

I had read about Lake of the Ozarks in the pages of *Bassmaster*. Seeing the signs off I-70, I drove south to an old, sleepy bait shop. The owner knew a local guide who could take me out the following morning. I found a cheap motel and stayed the night.

The bite had been tough that week with hot weather. Catching a few keepers was going to be a challenge, Gary told me when I stepped on the boat. We would catch spotted bass, but most would be shorter than 14 inches.

Gary took me straight to the best brush piles by docks, where I set the hooks of his homemade jigs into the piles one after another. He had to break them off with regret. His tone of voice and facial expression told me that he did not appreciate the time and effort lost on this neophyte.

I had to admit, my casting skills were rusty. My strength as an angler was never in being the best, but in learning and asking the right questions. I asked many questions that day and learned as I went, catching several spotted bass, as Gary had promised. Along with my questions came my eagerness to exchange stories and spin fishing tales.

Before long, Gary and I were chatting up a storm, and I had disarmed him with my naivety and my admiration for any fisherman who had more skill than I did. He caught a few keepers while I struggled catching the small ones. I didn't tell him about Castaic, but of course, my conversation headed to size and records. His record was only eight, he said, but it should be and would be 15. A pair of them. Both state records.

"Where?" I asked.

"Right here," he said. "One cove over, although I have never gotten them to bite."

"You can see them?"

"Not likely," he said. "The water's pretty clear now, but these fish sit in 15 feet of water right next to a big submerged tree. Typically, you have to scuba dive down to see them. That's how we found them the first time. I've only seen them roam the shoreline once."

"You're kidding."

"No. I'm for real." He was. I could see the honesty in the dark tan lines at the edge of his eyes.

Before I even had the chance to ask him, he was pulling up the trolling motor and putting on his life jacket to head over to the next cove.

"I've seen them three times while scuba diving," he said as we pulled into the cove. "The guy that found them has seen them at least six or seven times. I didn't believe him the first time he told me, since he is not a fisherman. He does scuba for fun and water skiing and stuff. When he took me down there, my eyes about popped out of my head." Gary let out a huge chuckle as he made a funny expression with his eyes bulging. I laughed.

"It hasn't rained for a month, and the water is so clear and low right now. If they are relating to that log, there is a remote possibility that we could see them. I haven't come by this way for a while."

The water sparkled with light ripples off the water at the entrance. Trees lined the shoreline. The water inside the cove was still and calm. Gary killed the engine and used the trolling motor the rest of the way in.

"The key is polarized sunglasses," Gary said.

He tied a new hair jig on the end of my line and put on a fresh piece of pork. "I doubt they will bite, but hey, why not try?"

His strategy was to cast the deeper edges of the spot first, where the fish likely had moved to avoid the hot sun, especially with the low water level.

We fished the jigs without a bite, and then moved in closer. Nothing.

Right up toward the bank, I could see the tree about 10 feet under the surface. Some bluegill darted away when the shadow of the boat covered their hanging spot. Then, far to our right, along the bank, I saw them. They were a giant pair of northern largemouth bass, cruising the shoreline as bass do, looking for an easy meal in six feet of water.

They swam right toward the boat, which had now drifted over their hiding place. When they saw us, they were not alarmed; they simply swam deeper. Gary's line was still in the water as he jigged the shoreline side of the tree. Mesmerized by the fish, I did not even say anything. I smiled to myself when I saw his serious expression as he worked his jig ever so slowly. The bass came up shallower once they passed the boat and continued down their stretch of shoreline.

I did not say anything to Gary about seeing the fish. My mind was formulating a live bait setup to catch those fish another time on my own.

When we pulled up toward the ramp, Gary gave me the pro guide's sermon I have heard a dozen times since:

"Well, we did pretty good today considering the conditions. We caught a few fish and learned some new techniques. We discovered that depending on weather and sunlight conditions, fish don't always bite or let themselves be caught."

He continued on, and I would not have been surprised if an announcer's voice was heard above saying, "And now for these messages from our sponsors."

I wondered how many hours he dedicated to fishing that one spot. He shared the fact that he would give up after some days with absolutely no luck. Others had likely seen those bass and tried in vain to catch them. Those Missouri state-record bass were no different than world-records. They are out there, but that does not mean that they are going to be caught. If they are caught, that does not mean that they will make the record books or that tackle sponsors will pay the successful angler. The "million-dollar fish," as they call it, might be a pipe dream. These fish are as elusive as they come.

Chapter 3

Crab Orchard Lake, Illinois

After spending a month or so with family, I began graduate
school in Southern Illinois. I inherited a small fishing boat from my
grandfather and docked it at the local lake, Crab Orchard. This
was my first chance to spend uninterrupted years on the water
and fine tune the art of bass fishing. I was a bit disillusioned with
the search for the world record, and I knew that no records were
to be found here, but I plugged away at learning new skills and
mastering my craft for the right time. I loved Southern Illinois, my
birthplace and fishing roots.

I spent countless hours on the water. I fished so hard that I
wore through all my equipment several times over a short span of

a few years. I made up for when I had wanted to go fishing and couldn't. Now I had to work a few hours at school a day and put out a newsletter once a month, and then I was free to fish. Winters in Illinois were horrible for me, though. That's when I spent all my time in fisheries research. As many hours as I spent in the biology building reading fisheries books, you would have guessed that my major was fisheries science—not literature.

I met Ray, the maintenance manager for the university, through my friends Greg and his girlfriend Jean. Jean had been telling me, "There's somebody you have to meet: Ray. He scuba dives and fishes, and he might even like fishing as much as you do." I was walking with Jean by the library when she spotted Ray coming from the biology building.

Ray was a stocky gray-haired man in his late 50s. We chatted for only a few minutes that day, but we spent hours on the phone and then in the boat, even in winter. If Ray could find water above 40 degrees, he could catch bass. He proved it the first time he took me out to Cedar Lake. I met him at the ramp as he was launching his aluminum boat with a 9.9 horsepower Yamaha.

He was the guide for the day, and I was his eager student. The sky was overcast, but 42-degree water with warm nighttime temperatures made it different from most days in February.

"Night-time temperature is more important than day-time temperature," Ray explained as we motored slowly to our spot. "Fishermen always look at day-time temperature and miss it because they fail to pay attention to night trends and how that affects the water overall. It takes at least two to three days for a water temperature change to positively improve the fishing this time of year."

He explained his approach to catching winter bass with his favorite soft jerk bait, a Mann's Shadow. While other bass fishermen fished a jig too quickly on the bottom, he was able to catch the winter suspended bass. We pulled up to his first deadfall tree, and he demonstrated his stealthy approach using spinning tackle and a slow, slow, slow retrieve. I had to follow his lead and make corrections as he pointed them out to me.

His Shadow was probably in 10 feet of water in front of the submerged tree when he reeled down the slack and set the hook on a three-pound bass. He fought it firmly and set his foot down on the trolling motor to motor farther away from the tree. A bass can easily break off eight-pound-test line on a tree limb.

He lipped the fish himself and held it up for me to see before releasing it.

He demonstrated the same technique again and caught another about five minutes later 10 yards farther up. I was mimicking his every move and was worried that I would not be able to duplicate his pattern. We came to the point following those two deadfalls, and I took the first cast to the shoreline.

We both saw a big swirl, and I could not believe a big bass would be that shallow in February. I reeled in the slack and set the hook firmly but with restraint. The resistance was as solid as it could be without breaking the line. The drag had been set perfectly.

Ray motored away from the point, and I held on with my rod tip high in the air. The weight was too heavy to reel with Ray steering us to deeper water.

Out in deeper water, I went to loosen the drag, and he stopped me.

"That should be right. Keep the pressure on and start reeling when you can."

I did slowly and was amazed by this fish's strength. After a few minutes, the fish was at the side of the boat, and Ray netted her in one fast swoop.

I laughed, astounded as he held the net and unhooked the fish. I said, "That has to be nine pounds or more!"

"No, it's eight two, maybe three."

I held it while he found the scale. He weighed it. Sure enough, eight pounds, three ounces.

Needless to say, after only a few hours on the water with Ray, he became my mentor. Much of what I learned about fisheries science started with conversations with him.

Soon after this trip, I was on Crab Orchard seeking out similar conditions in my boat, with my Mann's Shadow and eight-pound test line on spinning tackle. I found overcast skies and temps in the low 40s. Crab Orchard did not have any main lake deadfalls, but I hit main lake points with weed lines. I reasoned that these weeds draw more heat from the sun and act as a favorite ambush point. They also produce oxygen.

I cast out and let the Shadow sink with long pauses down about 10 feet. After a few casts, I felt a faint tick. I set the hook and connected to a solid fish. Mimicking my mentor's approach, I trolled the motor to deeper water. Trying to net a green, frantic fish too soon, I was lucky. The fish weighed eight pounds, four ounces.

Later on the phone with Ray, he said he had caught bass in the low eight-pound range every year, but had never caught one bigger than eight four. Some years he caught six or seven that big, but that seemed to be what the local waters could grow. That's what drew me into the science of making a bass become a behemoth.

Chapter 4

The Science of Growing Giant Bass

I spent most of my time in the library studying that month, but the topic was fisheries science—not Chaucer or Shakespeare. Sure, I did enough to pass my classes, but I became a zealot for big bass.

I learned the science behind what ingredients allowed bass to grow quickly, and I started to write out my own formula from the ground up, based on what I read from people like Doug Hannon and others in largemouth bass management.

Bass need quality water, but it does not have to be perfect. Some bass grow large in rather murky conditions, but some flow of water, proper oxygen levels, correct pH levels, availability of zooplankton and aquatic vegetation, and water temperatures of 55 to 75 degrees Fahrenheit make an ideal ecosystem for a bass. Water depth and stable conditions are important but are not the end-all. The end-all is food. Without adequate food, bass are never going to grow to be giants. This is the biggest mistake that people make when trying to raise a Goliath. They put in too many bass, and they do not put in enough food to feed all of them, especially in the years following spawns when the populations continue to grow. This is why most reservoirs lose their momentum in growing giants after about 12 years. The bass population is too large, and the food source is too small. With this knowledge, I developed my fish-to-food ratio. It became my sole study for months.

Bass love crayfish, shad, bluegill, smaller bass, and anything they can engulf in their big mouths. Bigger bass prefer an easy meal rather than chasing down many fast, small baitfishes. In a place like Florida with hot water temperatures in the 80s and 90s, bass have high metabolisms and cannot easily chase down enough food to grow to 25 pounds. The algorithm requires too much food. In 55 to 75 degree water, with high-protein foods like stocker trout, chub suckers, big shad, and crayfish, bass can grow huge. Add to this a strong genetic makeup, including a cross of a Florida-strain bass with a northern bass, and the result is a super bass. People have tried to do this and failed, but a few have made progress in this field, such as the Texas Freshwater Fisheries Center, where I would later travel and study.

I spent time with Ray and the biologists at Crab Orchard National Wildlife Refuge talking about their annual surveys. We even went out a few times and observed as they shocked some of the smaller lakes in the area. We spent half a day at the Little Grassy hatchery as well. Ray already had relationships with many of these locals. On one of these trips, Ray said he knew someone I should meet.

"I'm surprised you haven't run into her yet," Ray said.

"Why?"

He turned the corner toward the Little Grassy dam and smiled at me. "She is writing her master's thesis on spawning largemouth bass in Midwest lakes."

"You're kidding! Geez, I could write her paper for her." My thesis was on "Fishing in America: Hemingway, Maclean, and Duncan," focusing on the search for the elusive and the metaphor of fishing as religion in modern American fiction. If my thesis director would have allowed me to write on bass spawning, I would have done that instead.

"If you play your cards right, I'll introduce you," Ray kidded.

A few days later, he did. His building was right next to the biology building, and she spent all her time there in the lab.

"Jay, I want you to meet Lauren. Lauren, this is Jay, the fishing nut I told you about."

Lauren laughed and stood up to shake my hand. "I thought you were the fishing nut, Ray."

Lauren had strawberry blonde curly hair, blue eyes, and glasses. She looked like a scholar with a sexy country girl appeal. I found out later she was a farmer's daughter and a Missourian. I loved her charm and accent immediately.

I learned much of the science about fisheries from Lauren, but the kind of skeptical science of facts and numbers. Lauren knew nothing of the quest for the world-record bass that most big bass fishermen share. She knew the statistical components of what it takes for a Midwest lake to sustain fish and the natural conditions and habitat required. She thought I was more of a mystic than a scientist when I started talking about stocker rainbow trout and chub suckers.

"Rainbow trout do not belong in a Midwest lake," she argued. "What the fisheries biologists are doing at Devil's Kitchen is wrong. That lake was never meant to have trout in it." She was firm and outspoken about keeping fisheries natural and native.

I could not argue with her about science and her purist approach; she was true to an exacting methodology and saw everything in black or white, wrong or right. She did not see the possibility of what might be or take risks based on hunches as I did, and in that respect, we were opposites. We liked each other nonetheless and spent time talking and learning from each other. She let me read her thesis, and it was more boring than the Victorian-era novels required for one of my classes. She had graphs of data and statistics without any conclusions or clear analysis. None of it made any sense to me. She was a detail person, and I was a big-picture person.

In my thesis, I discussed Hemingway's early approach to seeking solace from his war-torn life through fishing. Fishing was much more than an escape; it was a pursuit of the elusive, for greatness, for what could be. Hemingway's later philosophy in *The Old Man and the Sea* made more sense to me. There is something heroic, yet ironic about the search for enormity in what is found—and maybe even lost—in fishing, in love, and in life.

Chapter 5

A Generational Fishing Legacy

We were so busy with our theses that I never found time to introduce Lauren to my grandfather, the man who taught me about fishing. I owe my inspiration for developing a new lake to my grandfather, C.J. Covington. He was a successful industrialist who started off in life building power lines across the Rocky Mountains with the aim of being the foreman of a plant. He grew the business and ultimately bought it and ran it for 40 years in Mt. Vernon, Illinois. His hobbies were trap shooting and fishing. This is where I caught the fever. Decades earlier, he devised a plan to build a lake where Rend, Illinois once stood. Now it is called Rend Lake. He came up with the idea and even went from club to club and from congressman to senator in pursuit of the support and funding to build it, which he eventually did as the Chairman of the Rend Lake Conservancy District.

One failed side venture in the project was a special three-acre lake developed for disabled people to fish. It had been designed to be a trophy bass lake, growing bass of "epic proportions." He had leading fisheries experts contribute to the project, so being offered a chance to fish the lake was a dream. I remember going there once with my dad. The Conservancy District had gated the property and only passed out a couple keys, including one to my grandad. I had one of the few keys in hand and thought, "This is it. This is the gate to the Illinois state-record largemouth bass."

As I made my first cast into the little lake with my crankbait, I expected my first strike to be the state-record bass. My heart beat quickly as I retrieved the bait. Suddenly, ping, I had one. Unfortunately, the tiny green sunfish was not much bigger than my crankbait. I cast out again and expected record results.

Again, I hooked a sinewy green sunfish the size of my four-inch bait. After about 10 more successive casts with the same results, I realized this was the crappiest lake I ever fished. When I say "crappiest," I don't mean that I caught a lot of crappies. The lake was loaded to the brim with stunted, aggressive green sunfish. Even at eight years old, I knew what a trophy bass lake looked like, and this wasn't it. A year later, fisheries biologists shocked the lake and verified what I had told my grandad a year earlier: the lake stunk.

The little lake may have been a flop, but Rend Lake was a huge success, not only for securing a viable water source for the Little Egypt region of Southern Illinois, but for tourism and recreation in the area. The main lake did indeed produce a state-record largemouth bass in 1982—but at the hands of a commercial net fisherman who harvested catfish and carp for pet food. The 16-plus-pound fish would have beaten the state record by almost three pounds.

All of this had an impact on me, so at the age of 22 when my grandad passed away, and I received my inheritance, I spent most of it on something that had become my quest to achieve the unattainable, my dream to raise and catch the world-record bass.

I read all the books and listened to all the experts about how to grow the world-record bass. I also listened to what Ray had to say about genetics. Then, I added common sense, faith, drive, a desire to do something truly remarkable, and filled in the missing links to build the world-record bass pond.

"Where?" I can hear every bass fisherman asking. "California?" After all, I was a Californian for 12 years. —No.

"Florida?" My dad lives there. —No.

"Illinois?" —No.

"Lake of the Ozarks?" —No.

"Georgia, the site of the existing world record?" —No.

Let me just tell you. —Kentucky.

"Kentucky?" Yes, I know. It's not far enough south and the climate is fairly cool in the winter. It has northern bass—not Florida strain or hybrid super bass.

Nonetheless, I chose Kentucky. The choice was based on the real estate market at the time and what I could afford. I stumbled into an opportunity to buy land that fulfilled all the requirements to build a world-record bass lake.

At Grandad's funeral, I had to think back to his story of Kentucky Lake and Blood River to make me smile. It also inspired me.

It was warm summer June night in the 1950s. No other sports writer landed the scoop on this. Now, almost 60 years later, it is a true story worth writing about.

Kentucky Lake was at its peak, and the B.A.S.S. circuit did not exist. The fishermen there were weekend and summer anglers on vacation. My grandfather, my grandmother, my aunt Pat, and her brothers Joe and Jon, were among them. This was the spot my grandparents chose to visit every June. My grandad spent the whole month pursuing bass.

Kentucky was hot and humid in June. You could sweat a quart of water or more per hour if you went out in the direct sun. Grandad quickly learned this and found he preferred evenings and nights better. After a few late-night stints with success, he did not spend as much time on the water during the day.

It took him as much as a week with a guide before he located the schools and discovered what they would hit. He then headed out on his own to enjoy the catching. My dad and uncle were not much into fishing unless it involved sandwiches and cookies. My aunt Pat was a sport and even went out for the whole night on a few occasions. On one of those hot and humid post spawn nights, my grandfather and aunt would win the Kentucky lottery, so to speak.

Grandad and a guide did all the work leading up to the catching episode. They located the schools of post-spawn bass and their feeding locations. Grandad did the nighttime work of *targeting their patterns. My aunt's first night out was a set-up she did not realize until years later.*

Grandmother did not ask questions when Grandad slept a long nap one June afternoon, and Pat did the same; she knew what they were up to. Grandmother had a lunch packed for them in the fridge when they headed out around midnight. Pat's young eyes were a bit blurry as she and her dad strolled down to the dock with gear in hand, but she had said she wanted to go, and her brothers wouldn't.

The crickets and frogs made a huge racket in the underbrush of the Kentucky Lake shoreline, thick with varieties of grasses and trees. Kentucky was a living, breathing entity in the summer, full of creatures, bugs, and chomping mosquitoes.

Kentucky was not known for big bass. The lakes in the region held northern largemouth bass of good size and some excellent Kentuckies, also known as spotted bass. River systems are also not known for trophy bass; in fact, the Tennessee and Ohio River Systems typically do not grow bass over five pounds. An eight pounder is considered a trophy of a lifetime. A six pounder is a hawg.

The night before, Grandad had caught two big bass and that's all, but they were brutes. He did not figure out the pattern until 4:30 a.m., but when he did, he had the feeling he could duplicate it and catch more, so he asked the kids to come along. Pat was the only taker. Even seeing the size of the bass did not convince Joe and Jon that they would be able to partake in the catching, nor did it interest them that much. They would rather sleep. Pat saw the size of the fish and knew she would be haulin' in at least her share. She had done a bit of "haulin' in" before. One of the bass that Grandad caught was teetering close to six pounds, and you don't often see fish that size. She knew, because back then, fishermen kept the keeper fish on stringers or else their wives thought they were lousy fishermen and providers. A man's catch was considered a measure of his worth.

The 14'2" aluminum boat got up on plane, and they headed out toward Blood River. The main lake had a slight breeze with a ripple on the surface. Grandad and Pat were the only people on the lake, with the exception of a few houseboats anchored off in quiet coves, unseen.

He turned toward the opposite side of a point where they started fishing medium-running baits.

"It seems like they started going crazy about 2:30. That's when I figured out top water would work. You can try it now, but I have not seen any action right off," he told Pat.

Pat threw toward the point. On the second cast, she landed a small white bass and threw it back.

"Not what we're looking for tonight, though if we were in a mess of them, I would eat 'em," Grandad said.

They fished for about an hour and only landed a few small ones. The water was flat and quiet on that side of the point. Pat paused for a minute. Then she saw and heard what he must have been referring to.

"There," Pat said. "On the other side of the river on that point. They're going crazy."

Grandad saw a few big top water explosions there. The bass started feeding on the adjacent point. They motored across the river, and pulled out the top water baits. Pat had a Jitter Bug for an even retrieve. Grandad had a Hula Popper. Both baits were made by Fred Arbogast.

Pat's bait hardly hit the water before a bass flew through the air, hooking itself in the side. She awkwardly pulled it in and strung it on the metal stringer. A fat two-and-a-half-pound largemouth, just about average. She had a feeling she would be throwing it back later.

Three or four pops of the Hula Popper and Grandad hooked a much bigger bass that sucked the lure off the surface. He had to play it, and it even pulled out drag. A four pounder. He was all smiles.

Pat did not take long watching her dad pull it in. Her bait was back in the water crawling across the point with extremely slow and measured speed. "Ka-booey!" The explosion of water was equivalent to a giant beaver flopping its tail in the water, but she realized a fish had taken her bait as her drag sang into the night.

Grandad laughed. Even in the dark, he could see the look of Pat's surprise and amazement at the strength of a bass. She was using braided line and a heavy rod, and the fish was pulling out drag—strongly! She quickly reeled it in after a couple of those short runs. Grandad's netting job was sloppy on this one. I still heard about it 50 years later. He must have banged into the side of the fish's head about six times before he netted the fish for her, a five and three-quarter pound fish, the biggest they had seen all summer, and Pat's personal record.

The crazy thing is…the action did not stop all night. They spent about two and a half hours on that point before it slowed down, and they moved to a third location. They had a big stringer of 20 fish, all largemouth, all hawgs of four to six pounds—not something anyone could shake a stick at in those days.

They were still on the first point when they started culling fish, not a common occurrence back then. Usually you caught your limit and went in, or more often, caught all you could catch and went in, tired of trying. When they left for the next point, the smallest fish on their stringer of 20 was slightly over four pounds. Pat had long ago thrown the two pounder back in. Grandad's best was six and a quarter, the first fish at the top of the stringer. It took a long time after that before he put down his rod and suggested another spot. The feeding frenzy had long since died out where they were.

"There was another spot about a mile from here where I saw something similar but didn't get to fish it," he said before pulling the cord of the Johnson outboard. They taxied over and threw out their top water baits on a long woody shoreline with erosion damage. Flooding had pulled huge trees into the river with the soil and made for some prime-looking bass haunts.

Pat's lure was stuck on a log before they had a chance to catch any. While untying her bait from the tree, she heard the first splashes down the way. Grandad rowed them closer to where they heard the fish start feeding. He tossed his Hula Popper well past the deadfall branches of a tree by its base, where the shoreline met the exposed roots. He popped it a few times along the trunk. Once his bait reached the sprawling branches, some of which jutted into the air, he paused. He let it sit there a while to drift a few inches naturally. When he was about to pop it again, there was a giant splash. Another six pounder! He pulled it in with only a few brush-ins with underwater branches. The fish would head straight for the deeper water if you let them.

Pat caught a few more, but none were big enough to cull a four pounder. She paused her Jitter Bug and started it again. It disappeared with a big swirl under the surface. The force of the fish was astounding.

Grandad netted the bass with only a few bangs to the fish's head this time. He laughed deeply and loudly. "Looks like you're culling another four pounder."

"How much do you think it weighs, Dad? Is it bigger than that other one?"

"Oh, sure. Seven pounds or better!"

Pat smiled. She could visualize her mom's face when she returned. She could show her the one she caught herself, big enough to make any angler back at the dock quite jealous.

The peak fishing came around 5:00 a.m. Same area, just as much action. Grandad now had the retrieve figured out. Cast to the base of the tree, pop, up a bit, pop, pause, pop, pause, pause, pause, pop, up the trunk, pop, up more, pop, reach the branches, long pause, HUGE POP!

The fish wrapped around a tree, and Pat had one arm around a branch with her fingers holding the line as she tried to pull it over while drag tore out. Suddenly, she dropped it and a big loose loop flew in the air. Grandad reeled frantically and held his rod tip high. The fish was hooked well. It stayed on.

Pat rowed to deeper water away from the snags while her dad gave instructions, as if she could do any better. His drag started to sing a bit here and there as the fish headed for its deepest run. It became simply a matter of time. Run, reel, run, reel, run, reel. The bass pulled up motionless at the end, making it *an easy job for Pat to grab it. She was better at netting anyway. She could stand up and see the fish's whole profile, even in the dark. It lay still in the bottom of the boat with the net around it. Pat stared at the size of it, significantly larger than her seven.*

"Wow," she said. "That's the biggest I have ever seen or even heard of. How big is it?"

Grandad smiled and wiped his brow and nose under his glasses from the sweat of the night. "Maybe not as big as one I caught at Lake Charles one time, but surely the biggest I've caught here. Maybe not nine, but eight something."

Pat went to take out the hook and remove the fish from the net but changed her mind when she saw its powerful tail lift up. Grandad clenched the jaw of the fish sternly and wiggled the treble hooks loose.

The bass froze motionless, glistening wet in the night air.

"I guess we can cull another four pounder."

Pat pulled up the stringer and found the smallest fish of the 20. She estimated it weighed four and a half pounds as she released it. Normally, that would be considered a "good summer" trophy—just one four pounder!

Grandad took the stringer as she handed it to him with great effort, most of the fish remaining in the water. Dragging it along had become an impediment now with the danger of it breaking off the side clamp of the gunwale. The stringer was not made for fish of this size. Pat had a bad feeling as her dad dropped the eight and three quarter pound fish into the water with the others.

The action was light at the tail end of their run as they neared the shallower water. They headed to their first point, where they had not seen much action initially. The sun peeked over the horizon in a magnificent display. Pat felt elated, despite being tired. Her stomach growled for the sandwiches they never ate. What would she tell her mom? "Forgot to eat," I guess.

She smiled and even laughed a bit to herself, imagining Jon at the other end of the fishing pole. She thought back to that smallmouth he caught trolling. His expression was sheer fear of *losing the fish. His chubby cheeks were serious up until that final moment when they poked out in a big grin as he held up that three-pound smallmouth.*

The sun was red, orange, and then yellow, all mixed together with a light pink as the sun came up over the water. The fishing was nearly dead at that point, and Grandad returned to a medium diver "just for fun."

"I think the action is about over," he said.

"Yeah, I agree. I'm about ready to go in whenever you are," Pat said, the words followed by a noticeable growl from her stomach as she imagined a warm pancake upon her return. Forget the dead cow sandwiches, she thought. I can say those were Dad's leftovers.

"Yep. Let's go," Grandad said, reeling his wet plug to the side of the boat where those big fish hung underneath.

Another boat rounded the corner of the point. One guy was in the front casting, and another guy was rowing. They must have only started fishing.

"Catch anything?" the guy on the bow asked.

Grandad restrained a big laugh. Pat could tell he wanted to say something, but that he wanted to maximize the moment. She reached down in the water and helped him as she could see he was going to pull up the stringer to leave. He lifted his side, and she grabbed one end too. They pulled it up together in one monumental effort.

"Oh, we caught a few," Grandad said loudly over their way, with as little emotion as he could.

The guy in the front of the boat dropped his jaw in wonderment; his tongue bugged out a little too as a reflex. His cast turned into some kind of freakish movement that more closely resembled a shot put than a smooth cast from a casting rod and reel.

The guy rowing saw the huge stringer of fish and stopped in disbelief. His astonishment turned to doubt and criticism. "What did you catch those with? Kentucky fishin' poles?" he accused, meaning dynamite, a common practice back in those days.

"No," Grandad said, dropping the huge stringer of fish on the bottom of the boat with a big effort. "Just those divers," he said. He held up his rod and stuck his lure toward them so they could see it.

"Oh, I see that's the same color your buddy's using. That's the one I've been usin' all night," Grandad lied.

One of their oars fell in the water as the guy reached for his pole and began a frantic slapping motion for a cast. It resulted in a backlash one might see after a child gets a hold of his old man's casting reel for the first time.

The other guy continued to cast successfully, but at the most frantic pace in the most erratic manner, almost to the point that his bait more or less skimmed the water like a dragonfly skimming across the surface of a Midwest pond.

As Grandad cranked up the motor and idled away from the point, Pat laughed, seeing the fishermen's oar floating away without their notice, while the guy in front tried in vain to pull line *out of the backlash. The other guy was fly casting with his bait caster to the speed of 30-plus miles an hour.*

Grandad leaned forward with an embarrassed grin as they now faced away from the other fishermen. "Those clowns are gonna get skunked if they can even keep their baits in the water long enough to say they tried."

Pat burst out laughing as her dad turned the handle full throttle, and they raced back home over the glistening sunrise-lit water.

I'll let the story end here, as there's not much to tell once they returned to the cabin with the others rolling out of bed. Jon and Joe's comments ruined the moment, and grandmother was mad about the uneaten sandwiches.

I had heard the story at least two dozen times from Grandad and at least a dozen simpler versions from my aunt, which inspired me to take a drive down to Kentucky a few weeks after the funeral.

I had been thinking about how I would build the ideal lake. I thought about all the flawed approaches the Crab Orchard fisheries team had taken. They tried to maintain balanced lakes with too many diverse species, including white bass, striped bass, hybrid striped bass, crappie, and even large trout. Stocking all those different species in competition with one another would never provide an environment for a record largemouth. With the right opportunity, I would create a lake that did.

As I drove through the hilly area around Lake Barkley, I stopped and picked up one of those *Country Real Estate* books with listings of land and farms. I came across a listing for an old hog farm with a creek running through it that captured my attention. My theory was in line with what Doug Hannon said, in that a trophy bass fishery would optimally include a clear stream of water with movement. Maybe a river system like the St. John's River in Florida without the pollution. In a smaller, more controlled environment, I could raise super bass, the hybrid between northern largemouth and Florida-strain largemouth.

I went to look at the pig farm. The property was useless (too hilly for farming) with abandoned sheds and pig troughs on top, and a runoff pond way down below at the bottom of the hill. Coming out of the hill was something much better than a stream though; I walked up and discovered a spring came straight from the side of the hill that formed the stream below the farm.

In that moment, I saw something that no one else would have: a 70-acre lake formed by bulldozing the gaps in three hills, with a small dam at the bottom on one corner where the stream exited the lower corner. The top of the lake would be hillside where the spring came out, with facilities and sheds not far off the top. The property did not even need much tree removal. The lower part of the area was marshy without any brush, shaded some by large oaks at the top of the hills.

On the way back to the university, my mind was racing with ideas. The following weekend, I called the real estate agent and made an appointment. I told Lauren about it, asking her if she wanted to come down there with me. She thought the idea sounded crazy. However, she was sympathetic about my grandfather passing and was trying to be comforting without being too critical of how I wanted to honor his legacy. When I explained it all to her and how my grandad built Rend Lake, she understood why I wanted to do something to memorialize him.

Chapter 6

Building My Bass Lake

The real estate agent met us at the property by the sheds, off the gravel road.

"It's a failed hog farm," she explained. "After the hog market crashed some years back, it foreclosed. It has gone through a few different agencies who have listed it, but there is not any interest in it."

"I can see why no one would have any interest in it," I said. "Without a house or any real usable buildings. The outbuilding for the pigs is not much value for anything else."

She showed us through the rickety structures. Lauren tagged along and listened. I asked the agent many questions that she could not answer. She said she would be glad to meet me back at the office, and she could check on them.

"Okay. I'll see you back at the office. I want to show Lauren the marshy area below."

"Fine. Look around some more. I'll see you later," she said, stepping into her vehicle.

I led Lauren down the hillside and pointed out the spring coming from the side of the hill.

"It makes the land down here unusable," she said.

"Yeah, right, unless you are going to build a lake."

She smiled. She had me figured out. She walked up to the water and felt it.

"A nice 55 to 58 degrees," she said. "That would make your lake unseasonably warmer during winter, especially at the top end here."

I showed her the places where I would dam up between the hillsides and where I would dam up the creek down below.

"That seems easy enough," she said. "The soil would be suitable for a pond. It already has a natural forage base with the marshy back ends that could act as brooding areas for juvenile fishes.

She started a lecture on how this ecosystem could naturally sustain itself with a marshy area where bass can ultimately breed. Those were the moments when I found her particularly attractive, and I was not listening much to what she was saying. Her conservative recommendations were an affront to my fantasy adventure of raising a trophy bass fishery, but her eyes were a perfect blue and her curls were gorgeous. I put my arms around her, and she was still talking hesitantly. I kissed her.

My plans for the lake went ahead smoothly, with the sale of the land going without a hitch at a steal. I had plenty of money for the whole construction project and for long-term stocking and development. I would build the dams immediately before spring rains. I did not have any trouble finding a couple of guys in construction who were out of work, and I managed the project myself. By the end of March, my crew dammed it, with a few areas of sand and pea gravel added. As Lauren pointed out though, it naturally had some variation in soil and clay.

Most fishermen who go about building a trophy lake do it backwards. They build a lake and start stocking a bunch of big bass immediately to catch them. This ruins the lake since the big bass eat all the food right away. Then those fish are starving months later without any food sources, vegetation, or areas for food to grow.

I probably would have made that same mistake too, given I am an impatient fisherman. The difference is that I was now dating a scientist, a purist about ecology and what it takes to sustain a fishery naturally. She insisted that I do it right.

"You have to let it fill up, then let the baitfish and aquatic vegetation proliferate and reproduce for at least two years," Lauren said to me one day at the lab.

"Two years? Are you crazy? I want some big bass in there later this summer."

This conversation went on for some hours before I came to my senses. I would also have to wait to implement my secret stocking plan. I would have to do it right, to provide the ingredients that the lake needed to grow the baitfish and to grow the vegetation and habitat needed to sustain them.

I gave the lake a whole season to grow some plankton naturally. We planted water willow and some other aquatic vegetation that was native to the region. The only baitfish I stocked in those first few months were crayfish I purchased from Mississippi. I created breeding areas and some feeding stations in the shallow, marshy areas. I built little mud castles with wooden pallets at several places along shorelines, where I placed groups of the crayfish. Lauren was not pleased with me about this since they were not native. That summer we stocked fathead minnows and some threadfin shad. This was Lauren's key suggestion for a Midwest lake that stays above freezing. Any farther north and the threadfin would die off some in the winter.

The few trees that had been removed were used as fish structures in the deeper spots of the lake, 12 to 24 feet deep. The deepest holes were dug there. We also manually created breeding boxes for the fatheads on some of the shallow shorelines with wooden crates where they could attach their eggs.

I noticed that by the fall, some tadpoles had hatched from the lake, obviously laid from frogs living in the muck of a drainage pond a few hundred yards away. Nature was going to take care of some food sources on its own.

By winter, I was out taking temperature readings at the top by the spring and found it to be around 50 degrees down deep there. That was in contrast to local lakes where surface temperatures could be in the upper 30s and deeper temperatures would be in the low 40s. Later, I would find ways to raise the temperature even higher during the mild winter months.

In the spring, I stocked bluegill and redear, two fish that are similar, but that live and breed in different areas and depths of the lake, so they would not be stunting each other's growth or crowding each other out. They had plenty of food by then, and I was confident about stocking them both, even though Lauren discouraged the redear. Ray had helped me with my approach, and he was on board with stocking the redear.

After the hatchery truck left that day, I walked along the shoreline of my lake and imagined the giant bass that would one day be thriving there.

I walked to the top of the lake by the hillside where the spring came in. I looked over the still, shady water and was certain that this would be where my biggest bass would live, near the warmer water in the winter. I wondered what might lurk beneath these depths one day. Suddenly, I noticed a big bubble come to the surface right in the middle of the small cove in front of the spring. A few other bubbles followed. In the stillness of the spring afternoon, it seemed like the bubbles made some noises as they reached the surface. I imagined that they came from air pockets in the spring water. It made me think of a passage I once heard. I remembered it as something like this: "Deep calls to deep at the noise of the waterspouts. All the waves and billows flow over me." I imagined that is how the bass would feel down there, at least.

My strategy for my lake development focused solely in doing whatever it takes to raise the biggest bass. I listened to Lauren on a couple small points and did not stock crappie. Even though bass will eat crappie, the species can overtake a lake and start competing with the smaller bass. I knew that could be a huge risk in stunting the growth of any juvenile bass. I also decided not to stock catfish. Almost all would stock catfish immediately since they are a prized food source, but I did not want catfish to interfere with what I was trying to do for the bass. Channel catfish are aggressive predators who can grow to giants, and I did not want them competing against my prized bass, even though their diets are somewhat varied.

Instead, in the second season, I stocked chub suckers, a costly and timely endeavor based on a hunch I had from some stuff I had read by Florida biologists about the best bass fisheries in the south. One biologist wrote a paper about how all the fisheries with the chub suckers grew bass of extraordinary size. Because these fish are long and soft, they are a perfect meal for a big bass. They do not evade capture easily and do not overtake a lake since they do not breed successfully there. I stocked what I could find at a high cost, spending more money than all my stocking efforts prior to this.

Lauren looked over a chub sucker in a bucket from the hatchery truck from down south. "$3.50 for one of these. What were you thinking, Jay? Why not some more shad?"

"Well, yes. I am going to add more shad, of course," I said.

To me, the tanned and yellow chub sucker, long and skinny, looked like a filling and delicious meal. I was a fisherman who had learned to think like a big bass. Lauren was a fisheries scientist.

Lauren became enraged with me late in the second season. Instead of stocking fingerling northern largemouth bass as she instructed, I had taken a radical approach by stocking the expensive crossbred super bass from a hatchery further south. Most of them were 10-14 inches. A few were even bigger. I stocked fewer bass than they recommend for a 70-acre lake though. This is another thing I did that others, especially trained fisheries people, would not do. I stocked the ratio I had figured out in my own algorithm for growing the most incredibly-sized bass—not for yield or numbers. The bass I stocked would have at least three times as much food as what they might have in someone else's pond. Even after Lauren's objections, I installed fish feeders to spread out high-protein feed twice daily, to continue supplemental feeding of the farm-raised bass for a year or two. I could later use the feeders with some smaller feed for my secret winter stocker, rainbow trout. Lauren argued that the baitfish I had already stocked were adequate; all these other efforts were unnecessary. For my purposes, these deviations from traditional fisheries science were my means to an end: the world-record bass.

Now that I had a lake with some super bass in it, no matter how small they were, my mind started churning faster and faster with more ideas for stocking. Soon I had figured out how to convert the pig troughs into fish runways to create my own fish farm to save money and create a huge volume of feeder fish. Rainbow trout and chub suckers were my first attempts, since I knew those would be the high-protein meals that a giant bass would require. This had already been proven with the rainbow trout stockings out west. Every month in the news, California anglers caught another trophy in those lakes.

I transplanted shad from Baldwin Lake and also purchased some from a southern hatchery. The shad would eat plankton, reproduce, and proliferate all summer. The bass were essential to keep their numbers in check. Occasional restocking of shad was part of my plan though, because I had already seen how the guys at the Crab Orchard National Wildlife Refuge did not keep some of the smaller lakes, like Devil's Kitchen, stocked well enough with shad. To me, this was a key ingredient.

With reluctance, Lauren helped me with the runways and with fine-tuning the water temperature and filtration. I killed plenty of fish those first few months, but I was smart to put some in the lake right away as well. I was hoping to do some of my own stocking at the right times when the bass grew bigger, so I could stock fish in the right size slot, such as a five-inch rainbow trout, and later on, a six-inch chub sucker. This would also require a large volume of fish, which I could not afford at $3.50 per fish. My fish farm operation was more successful than I could have hoped. Early that spring of the third season, we decided to shock the lake to see how the bass were doing and what they could eat.

Lauren brought a small research boat from work that we could carry over to the lake from the trailer. I never built any kind of a boat ramp. This was not a fishing lake, after all. At least not yet.

Ray and Lauren led the survey since they had both participated in many over the years. In fact, I did not even go out with them. I watched from the shore. They said I would become too excited in that little boat and interrupt their study. I watched from the sidelines on the sunny April day, where bass could be seen making wakes in some areas, where they had come up to feed.

The first bass shocked up was about two and a half pounds. "Hey, great job, Jay. That's excellent growth over the winter," Ray said across the lake. They shocked some other spots further down in shallower water out of sight.

Back at the shoreline, Lauren kneeled on the bow, and I caught her as she jumped to the shore. "Hey, thanks, you two, for doing the survey. How did we do?"

Ray said, "Pretty good, really, Jay."

He climbed out and pulled out his clipboard. "Twelve bass, all two to three pounds. All healthy and fat. That and two green sunfish."

"What?" I asked, alarmed. "How did they get in there?"

Lauren said, "Birds. They are going to get in no matter what you do here."

"Did you kill them?" I asked.

"No, why?" Ray asked.

"Those green sunfish are a nuisance. They can compete against the juvenile bass."

"Aww, they are natural," Lauren stated objectively. "The bass can eat them."

"I hate them though," I said.

"No worries," Ray said. You should be able to start stocking your rainbow trout soon. Those bass will be big enough to eat some smaller trout.

Lauren had kind of a disgusted look on her face as we pulled up the boat and loaded it back on the trailer.

When we arrived back to Illinois, I kept thinking of more ways to increase the food ratio for my fish. I decided I would fertilize the lake and put in some more shad in a few weeks. My mind stayed focused on my one objective. Finishing out the semester and spending time with Lauren were secondary considerations.

Chapter 7

A Weekend at the Lake

I could tell that Lauren was unhappy with all the time and expense I had put into the lake. Fisheries science was a job to her and not something she looked forward to on the weekends as an escape. She stressed over problems that her advisor pointed out in her thesis. Ironically, he was dissatisfied with the "lack of lab and field work" she had put into the project and had asked her to continue her work on a couple fronts. The weeks ahead would be a lesson in reality. School would be over, and we would be off looking for real jobs. Our leases would be up at the end of the month, and we would have to figure out our next move. Ray was moving to Florida for retirement in his camper. He had already started packing.

He called me Saturday morning. "Can you come to my place with your truck? I have a gift for you. Bring some tie-downs."

"Tie-downs?"

"Yeah, straps. You'll need them. In fact, bring your boat trailer too."

"What? With my boat?"

"No, without the boat."

I showed up at Ray's, curious. Out front, his camper was loaded up with his little boat on top. His driveway was covered with a huge blue mass of what appeared to be plastic.

I saw him come out the front door. He pointed to the driveway.

I laughed. "That? What is it?"

He walked over to it and picked up one edge. "It's an Olympic-sized pool cover."

"It's huge!"

"It's 50 by 25 meters."

"What's it for?"

"Your lake, dummy. Don't you want to warm up the top end by your spring?"

I paused and looked at it closely. The insulated pool cover was composed of many little bubbles, almost like bubble wrap. I smiled. The bubbles acted as an insulator.

"It will keep the temperature up in the winter by retaining heat from the warm water of my spring in the winter. In the summer, it can keep the temperature down from the direct rays of the sun and shade that area," I said.

"Yeah, maybe as much as five, six, seven degrees in the winter. A lot more if you put in a small heater at the bottom right by the spring."

"My god, you're starting to think like a power plant maintenance manager," I said. Ray knew what I meant without saying it. Lake of Egypt was only ten miles away, heated by the warm water discharge of a coal-burning power plant. A 16-pound bass was caught and landed there once but was never submitted as a state record. A plant maintenance worker caught it in the restricted area. We fished the lake a few times, but it had too much fishing pressure. It did not have enough food for the fish to grow to trophy size. It had many fish under the slot limit—the opposite of what I wanted to achieve. All lakes will grow a few trophy fish if a few of the bigger fish can hurdle to the point where they can eat stunted 10-inch bass.

"Thanks, Ray. I can't thank you enough."

"Hey, no problem. It was trash. The hassle was hauling it over here before it was picked up and sent to the landfill. It only has a few issues. Nothing that duct tape and zip ties won't fix. For your purposes, this is golden." He smiled. "It's going to be a slow drive to your lake with this."

"Hey, when are you leaving?"

"In a week. My kids are going to sell the house. I'm going to travel around. Camp, fish, that kind of thing. What about you and Lauren?"

"I don't know yet, but I guess I have to start applying for jobs in order to support my habit," I half joked. I was talking about my fish feeding habit, which had become an expensive endeavor. In contrast, I had not spent much time or money dating Lauren or thinking about our future.

Ray did not catch my dry joke and was focused on sharing his final advice. "You better get that cover on and strapped down somehow, at least before next winter. I would put it on by summer and let it be a shade area for the summer months too. I think it will help your trout survive then as well."

"Excellent idea, Ray."

"You might consider calling Pond Boss and fertilizing the lake too, if you can afford it. You want the water to be rich with plankton for those shad. If you keep that up, they will have food and will proliferate. You won't have to stock them as much."

"I had decided on that, but I don't want it to grow a bunch of nasty algae either."

"So far, so good on that. You can always add an aerator at the shallow end this summer to curb growth."

I couldn't wait to load the cover and take it to the lake. Ray helped me, and I was headed back to Kentucky.

When I arrived at the lake, I walked down the hillside and around to the most open area. The sun was bright, bringing the temperature to 74 degrees Fahrenheit. The birds were singing, and the lake was swirling with activity. I saw bluegill sunning themselves in the shallows and darts from some bass here and there. I saw one big bass swim by toward a school of bluegill. That had me running back up the hill to my truck for a two-piece rod.

Walking back down the hill, I thought to myself, "This will be my first fish from my lake!"

I crouched down to keep a low profile and watched fish swim by for a while longer. In the distance, a school of shad popped to the surface for a spell. I only saw one blowup on the shad, but imagined other bass were feeding deeper down.

I didn't have much tackle with me, but tied on a medium-diving crankbait in a brown color. I tossed it as far out as I could and reeled it steadily. Nothing. To my right I saw a bass take out some bluegill. I cast that way. Nothing.

I fished for about 20 minutes before I thought to myself, "All this food, and they are not going to want artificials."

About an hour later, I saw the school of shad swim closer with more blowups. I cast right to it this time. Bam! My first strike. The fish pulled out some drag, fought hard, and jumped twice close to the shoreline before I was able to lip it. A solid three pounds, maybe some change. Fat, but could be fatter, especially this time of year.

I decided right then and there. I would call the pond management guy to spray the deeper half of the lake with fertilizer. If it gummed up the shallow end toward July, I would install an aerator there. I would also order a heater for October installation. I would stock more shad.

I walked back to my fish building to see how my stocker fish were doing. As I walked by the deep pool by the spring of the lake, I saw the bubbles again. I was too far away to hear the noises, but I imagined them.

In the hog shed, the trout looked sleek and frisky in the aerated water. I only found a few dead, of hundreds in three runways. I refilled the feeders and hand fed them too. They were two to three inches. One runway had some bigger ones, three or four inches. I would probably start dropping a bucket of them into the lake within a month or so by my feeding stations, where hopefully, the bass were still picking up pellets.

I checked on my baby chub sucker runway. Lauren had been successful in getting brood stock, and they were all hatched and alive. Several hundred tiny chub suckers swan around. They would grow, and I did not need them yet anyway. This would save me thousands when the time came. I was already low on money.

The heater and aerator were going to be expensive, not to mention fertilizing the lake. The guy would probably tell me it takes at least a couple applications too. I knew that, and I was willing to spend whatever I had to in order to achieve my goal of growing shad and feeding my bass. I had to do it to avoid spending days hauling food. A trip to Baldwin was a pain, and most shad died during the trip. Even the hatcheries were not always successful transporting threadfin. I wanted to get away from using hatcheries. It is always a risk to bring in fish from other places, with diseases, viruses, and the like. Lauren had warned me numerous times.

I walked out the back and along the northern shoreline of the lake by two of my feeders. I refilled them and waited for them to turn on. They went on right before dusk, and I waited. Bluegill popped up first. Then I saw redear. They were the most eager feeders, and they were all at least three to six inches. The smaller ones hung more toward the bottom trailing up the remnants. Then came the bass, but they were pegging the redear and bluegill. Good, bad...I don't know, but my mind was back to the drawing board. Those redear cost almost 50 cents each from a hatchery. If bass were tearing them up like this, they were not going to last. I knew the bluegill would last and reproduce well. They do in every lake.

I saw a few bass eat the pellets, but I figured out the issue. Why eat a small pellet when you can peg a five-inch fish? In all, my strategy was working. I would feed them myself right here at my stations. If I could find a cheap fish hatchery to stock golden shiners, then that would be significantly cheaper than feeding them redear. Golden shiners were extremely affordable and proliferated more quickly.

I slept on the cot in the old pig shed that night, which was a little cold. The next morning I headed for some breakfast in a nearby town, then came back for some more fishing. I caught one big redear on my crankbait, which I threw back immediately. Those big redear and bluegill laid thousands of eggs, creating an abundant food supply for the bass. I caught a skinny two-pound bass and kept it. I realized that I would have to harvest some fish too. I was not going to be able to raise hundreds of trophy bass. My goal was to raise some trophies and weed out the rest. Once bass started spawning, that would create more food.

In my trailer back at the wildlife refuge that night, my answering machine was blinking. I battered my fish in Cajun seasoning and deep-fried it in vegetable oil. I ate it steaming hot, and I was satisfied. Maybe I would answer the angry messages from Lauren tomorrow.

Chapter 8

Lake Fork

I listened to my messages, and Lauren was wondering where I was and why I had not called to do something fun together. To me, the fisheries work was fun. She wanted an escape from the fisheries work and a boyfriend who would take her out now and then. I called her and reassured her.

"Can't I see you on campus later?"

"Sure, I'll be in the library studying. Find me there at my normal spot."

When I arrived, I bent down, kissed her, and gave her a hug. I could tell she was stressed and worried about school.

"Hey, you'll do fine," I said.

"I'm not worried about my finals; it's my research work and thesis. He pretty much wants me to start over."

"Well, you can do that as it comes. Just finish your finals. I have a final to give my students this morning and one later for American literature."

"Maybe we can meet for dinner later on."

"Sure." I kissed her and went to class.

Later on, we chatted over dinner at the Corner Diner. Lauren was in a better mood.

"So, what are you going to do next? Isn't your lease up too at the end of the month?"

"Yeah. I can continue my research work anywhere now. I don't have to be in the lab. He wants me to go to Lake Fork and study there for a week. That will be a drag."

"Are you kidding? That will be an opportunity! Can I come?"

"Sure, I thought you were going to get a job."

"Well, yes, I was going to get around to that. If I find some teaching jobs, classes won't start until the fall. In the meanwhile, I will finish my thesis and look for work. I might have to look somewhere like St. Louis. Logan College does not need any instructors right now."

We finished dinner and headed back to our respective rentals. Lauren had seen my place once and said it was a pit. It had two bedrooms, but one room was wall-to-wall tangles of fishing tackle. Hey, the rent was only $150 a month and the road was off the beautiful National Wildlife Refuge, within minutes of my docked boat. What more could an angler ask for?

In the following weeks, I packed up. Luckily, I found work starting in August at Southwestern Illinois College as an adjunct. Lauren found a job as fisheries curator at the St. Louis Children's Aquarium as it expanded to a new full-scale facility. I received a fall defense date for my thesis.

Lauren and I headed to Lake Fork for her field project before she started her new job. Observing the beautiful spring day in Southern Illinois, I imagined my bass would be on their beds spawning in Kentucky. I could see them prepping those sandy spots into round areas, their tails red and a little bloody from their work. I could see those stubborn males guarding those nests from bluegill and other intruders. Then, fat females would be twirling around beautifully, their white bellies sticking up toward the sky at times, a ritualistic dance of nature.

Lauren interrupted my dreams of spawning by asking me to sing a country song that was on the radio. I sang along, looking back at the research boat now and then to be sure all the equipment was still secure (including my rods and reels) as Lauren drove.

I became excited about the trip, thinking about the fishing and the giant bass spawning. Then again, the bass spawn was probably over in Texas. She was going to work with them in follow-up on post-spawn bass behavior and condition of the fish. I was annoyed that we were going to the Texas Freshwater Fisheries Center first since I had fishing fever and yearned to catch a few. Lauren had to meet with some of the fisheries scientists at the Texas Parks and Wildlife Department. Her advisor had been working with them, and they had agreed to share some important aspects of their spawning research with Lauren to help with her project.

The next morning we arrived at the Texas Freshwater Fisheries Center, meeting some of the staff there who Lauren would be working with. We introduced ourselves, but we never provided any details on what I was doing there, besides the fact that I was also from Southern Illinois University. Even though this was Lauren's project, I ended up asking most of the questions; this was my passion—not Lauren's.

I studied the tanks and layout of the facility. The setup was much simpler than I had assumed. I imagined something like you might see in a science fiction movie. This place had steel tanks and concrete floors, but much cleaner than my sheds. The building was enormous and contained an aquarium. The outside facilities included a big outdoor rainbow trout pond, tourist attractions, and numerous small research lakes. As the discussions among the scientists became more specific and technical, relating to their post spawn study, I lost interest and found myself alone in front of the big aquariums, staring at the bass. I did not see the giant bass I was expecting. The biggest I saw was maybe 13-14 pounds and spawned out. After a day there, I was glad to hear we were going to Lake Fork next and would be able to shock up some post-spawn fish.

I imagined the Lake Fork area to resemble Southwest Texas: dry and arid with tumbleweeds. To my surprise, East Texas was green and lush with trees and vegetation, more like Illinois than what one thinks of as the Southwest. As we drove over one of the bridges that cross the lake, I could see the abundance of submerged hardwoods, cedar trees, and standing timber. In addition, I saw lily pads, reeds, bull rushes, hyacinths, and several types of grass. It would be the model for my lake.

By 10:00 p.m., Lauren had explained the plans for the following day. Her prep work was serious, and I quickly lost interest. She was meeting with two biologists. I half-listened as I spooled up line and tied on the plastic lizards I had bought at the local tackle shop. The next morning I was out of bed and out on the point down from our motel before Lauren woke up.

The sun rose over the lake with pink and yellow hues behind the shadows of the standing timber. My morning pattern had failed, and nothing worked for me, but around 10:30 or 11:00 a.m., I had one of the best fishing experiences of my life.

Walking back from the point, along the shoreline, I cast out my Carolina-rigged lizard as far as I could into submerged grass. I dragged it along a few times. Then I felt a fish start to swim away with it. I set the hook and fought in a big bass easily weighing seven pounds. For a spawned out fish, it was still somewhat fat.

A couple casts later, the same thing happened. Cast, drag, drag. Then I felt a fish take up the bait and swim off. Bam, hook set. The fish jumped a few times. Another seven pounder and some change. Ten yards further down the shoreline, the same thing happened again, but I could see the fish in shallower water. That one weighed six and a half.

A little farther down, I landed another fish. The water was deep with a big tangle of submerged vegetation. My heart almost failed me, thinking I had a new state record. Finally, I dragged in the fish, weeds, and all. After unburying it, I saw a solid eight-pound fish, with almost as much girth as length, definitely the fattest fish I have ever seen anywhere. Maybe some of the fish still were on beds; I could not tell, but I was excited. By then, the sun was right overhead, and the fish buried themselves in the cover. I was hungry, so I found the nearby hamburger stand, ate, and went back to the room to sleep for a while. I dreamed of my fantasy day at Lake Fork in the boat with one of the pros, catching fish after fish, all 10 to 13 pounders, all top water, explosions of water that made your heart leap. Right then, I heard a slam. It was Lauren.

"Didn't you say you were gonna fish all day? You're sleeping?" She asked.

I shook off the dream and sat up. "I was fishing, out there and in my dreams."

"Catch anything?"

"In real life, on the point out here, yes, six to eight pounds. I don't think there are any fish under six pounds here at all! In my dreams, there was nothing smaller than 10 pounds. That would be considered a dink."

"Well, we shocked up plenty of small fish: sand bass, bluegill, crappie, tiny bass, you name it. Nothing over three pounds."

"That's not going to help you much in your study. Did the guy take you to proven spots?"

"I thought so. Lots of weeds, trees, and such."

I thought to myself. I bet they did not shock spots deep enough for post spawn fish. These scientists did not know anything about targeting fish. I kept my thoughts to myself.

"Maybe tomorrow if you aren't going out with them again, I can take you out and help you target some post-spawn bass."

"Sure, that would be helpful."

"What about tonight. Any plans?"

"No, I was thinking dinner."

"What about fishing 'til dark, then dinner?"

Lauren rolled her eyes at me and smiled. "I thought you would say that. In fact, I parked right by the ramp across the lot."

We walked across the lot to the ramp, one armful of rods and the other with a tackle box. Maybe I wasn't a girl's dream, but I was definitely living my dream.

We motored out of the cove and around to Big Mustang. Right around the corner, I saw a deeper weed line to target. "Here, I said."

"But this is almost main lake. Fish spawn in the coves."

"Big bass always relate to open and deep water, especially after a spawn," I explained.

Lauren had on a spinner bait, and I had on a jig with a plastic craw trailer. She cast along the weed line first as she was in the front of the research boat. She hooked a solid fish. "Two and a half pounds," she said, after weighing it carefully, as if we were in the last minutes of a tournament and had to cull within an ounce or so.

Three or four casts into my fishing, I let my jig sink down to the bottom in 15 feet of water. A light thud, pause, and I set the hook. "Aw darn," I said. "I think I hooked a stump. I'll have to break it off."

"Ha, ha, you stupid know-it-all," Lauren said. Right then, I felt my "stump" give way. Obviously, I had dislodged a hooked hawg from behind a stump.

"Ha, ha," I said. "I change my mind. This stump has become a fish!"

"What?"

"Don't 'what?' me. Get the net."

I would have steered the boat to deeper water if I had been at the trolling motor, but Lauren was now digging out the net, and I had to steer the fish out with my rod, away from the standing timber in front of the weed line. I steered her to the other side of the boat, with a couple hard runs underneath, where I was sticking my rod.

"Wow," Lauren said. "That is a big fish."

Right then, we saw it surface 10 feet from the boat. Its head was huge, and its gut bulged too much, not allowing it to jump.

Lauren kneeled and stuck the net out as far as she could. I dragged the fish right along the surface as the fish relaxed for a second right into the net. She lifted it out at the right time.

"Nice netting, Lauren. She was still green and ready to go again. I could have lost her." I lipped the huge fish and saw the hook of the jig was attached to the inside wall of the fish's mouth to a torn flap of skin—no bone or cartilage at all. In a few seconds more of fighting, the fish would have been lost.

Lauren had the scale in hand, and I put it on. "And the tournament director says, 'Eleven pounds, four ounces!'"

Lauren looked at the numbers and the fish with a stunned look, her mouth open. She was still staring when I released the fish.

"What?" She asked. "What about a picture? What about measurements?"

"Shoot! I did not even think about that. I was still in my dream, where this was one of the smaller fish. I had a kid take some pictures of me earlier today," I told her.

"You dummy. That was a big fish. You should have taken a picture."

"Sorry, I was thinking about the fish. This is a research vessel. Have to let her go right away."

"The fish can be out of the water for quite a while without any problems. We have to weigh and measure all those fish that we shock. That takes some time, but they are all fine when we release them."

"You're right. I guess I was anxious."

Lauren had her spinner bait back in the water, and I was still enjoying the moment, shaking a bit from the excitement, and fishing too fast now to catch a post-spawn bass on my jig. The sun started going down, and we motored back to the resort and trailered the boat.

We found the local steakhouse and relished in the stories from our day. Other raccoon-eyed fishermen filled the restaurant. I bit into the medium rare steak, and it melted in my mouth. I had never tasted a steak so fresh and tender.

Chapter 9

The Shock of a Lifetime

That night Lauren kept droning on about my fish and how she wished she had tagged it or measured it. I fell into a deep sleep while she was still talking about it. Lauren's exacting scientific mind kept working long into the night, while my dreams of spawning bass and giant catches returned.

We were in the boat by dawn the next morning to shock the same spot. Standing timber lined the corner. I could see some grass coming out of the water near the shoreline. A guide in Florida had once told me that if you can find a spot where three types of cover converge, you will find bass.

We shocked that point and around that corner about three times, but I did not see anything come up. Lauren saw a crappie or two, she said, but they did not come up to the surface. They hung stunned in the water column, about six feet under, where she could see them, suspended on their sides, then with their bellies up, almost as if they were dead, but with their fins fanning lightly to try to right themselves.

We went farther in and shocked a secondary point in the cove with success. Several bass in a school came right to the top. We both netted fish. Lauren went to work right away on the biggest fish with the measuring and weighing, while I held the other two in one of the live wells. She even took a tissue sample quickly. "Six, three," She said, holding it at the side of the boat to revive it. The other two were in the four-pound range.

We had more of the same, all day long. We shocked up bluegill, crappie, sand bass, small bass, and bigger bass up to seven pounds.

I could tell Lauren was tired and maybe a bit frustrated. "That's better than yesterday, but I was hoping for some fish in the 13 and up range for my study."

I thought for a few minutes. "Can you increase the current on your shock? I can see on the controls that SIU customized this boat. If you can, we could shock some of the bigger fish out in the deeper haunts."

"We're not supposed to," she said. "But you're right. This boat is custom designed to do all kinds of survey work, including killing Asian carp on the Illinois River."

I said, "Well think about it. If those bigger fish are on the bottom and you apply a greater shock, you are not going to hurt anything because they are not in six feet of water suspended. They are closer to the bottom already. I mean, you can see six to eight feet down right now. You will know that it is safe before you do it. This is not Crab Orchard after a big rain. The water is clearer here in these main lake spots."

She thought for a few minutes. "You know, that makes sense. I know that is why we don't shock at greater charges, so we don't hurt them, but if they are 18-20 feet deep, they will not be hurt.

We tried it. Most of the fish we shocked up did the same thing as that crappie. They were stunned and came up the water column, but most of them were out of reach. I saw this with catfish, carp, and some bigger bass to eight pounds.

"I have another idea," I suggested. "Let's hit some points with all the cover in around 10-12 feet of water instead of 20-25. With thicker grass and better cover, we might net a few in those conditions."

"Sure. Let's do it. Where to?"

I studied the map and directed her to some points farther north. The first one we found had perfect cover with trees, grass, a couple lay downs, and surface debris that all converged at a main lake point. "Go ahead and I will be ready with the net extended, already in the water."

She did, and I saw an eight plus float up the water column under a weed mat. She trolled over, and I netted it.

She weighed, measured, sampled, and tagged this one. Eight pounds, nine ounces.

We worked like this for about six days from dawn to dusk. We did not even bring the fishing poles with us. I became fascinated with this. I also saw how difficult it is. It is a fisherman's dream to go out and shock up the fish, but it's not that easy. We shocked up hundreds of fish, but most of them were small, even in the primo spots. As the weather warmed that week, I knew that the bigger fish were swimming deeper.

Finally, we shocked up a giant right at dusk in the same area where we found the eight-pound fish. I was able to net it, almost falling out of the boat in the process.

Lauren let out a victory yell. After days of this work, finally, success.

The fish weighed 12 pounds, 14 ounces, shy of being a fish that they would accept for the ShareLunker Program. After two more days on the water, Lauren was happy with our work and ready to conclude the study.

We gathered two types of grass for my lake in Kentucky and wrapped them in big hefty black trash bags for the trip home. We loaded up the truck and boat and retired for the night to head to Kentucky, then Illinois in the morning.

I could not sleep. I kept thinking about my lake and the size of the fish there compared to here. I wished that I could have that 12-pound fish in my lake. I also wished that Lauren could have shocked up a few more big ones for her study. I thought about what we did wrong and right, and then came to one of those "Aha!" moments. Those fish came up to the shallows at night to feed. We were not going to sample them in 20 feet of water. We had to wait until after midnight. I looked at the clock—12:05 a.m. My mind raced.

I found myself backing the boat into the water on the boat ramp. The jog north was dangerous at night. The boat navigated in and out of coves with the standing timber, but I found the best route in the moonlight.

A 10-minute trip north, and I was there. I shocked the inner weed line first. I couldn't believe it when a big fish came right to the surface in front of me. I netted it.

The fish was about the same size as the one we shocked up a few days earlier. Its head was huge with a bulging gut too. I looked for a tag. Nothing. It could have been its twin. I filled up the live well and put her in. Boy, Lauren would be happy and surprised!

I shocked up fish for about four hours. Fish of all sizes came up. Stacks of four pounders!

I tried the opposite side of the cove, where we had not yet shocked. It did not look as fishy, but sometimes, you don't always see the underwater cover that is abundant. Three or four shocks went without success. I went a little deeper, and ratcheted up the current one notch past what we had done in the past week. If it had been a moonless night, I would have seen nothing. However, in the corner of my eyesight, I saw the glistening side of a fish floating upward in the water column with a huge girth three feet under. I trolled over as fast as I could with the net in hand and let the boat drift quickly. I put the net under the water, and without spooking the fish, I took a strong underhand sweep toward the fish. The movement startled the fish, causing it to swim away and downward, but, with all my strength, I pulled it in. The fish was pinned flat on its side, and I pulled it and the heavy net up. The fish did a fast swimming motion, beating her tail against the aluminum bottom of the boat with a loud and forceful thumping. My heart leapt! The bass was a mature female, almost as fat in girth as she was in length. She was beautiful and perfect in every way. Like other giant bass that had been given "E" names like the famous "Ellen," I would name her "Elise." This is what Lauren was looking for; she would be so pleased with me.

On the way back to the launch ramp, my heart was beating fast. I could not think straight. I was trying to figure how much that fish might weigh. Sixteen? Seventeen? Twenty? I don't know, but the bass was enormous. I could not wait to wake up Lauren and tell her.

When I walked in the room, the sun was coming up. I made plenty of commotion, so I would wake up Lauren. She roused and growled faintly.

"Were you out fishing?" she asked angrily. She looked up at me with half-closed eyes.

"Yeah, I was..."

"You didn't use that boat, did you?"

"Well, yeah..."

"That boat belongs to the state of Illinois..."

"But, we used it to fish," I said.

"No, but you were out with me conducting research—not fishing for fishing's sake, you idiot! You can't go out in it—you are not designated by the university—you're not even on the insurance..."

Her criticism continued, but I stopped listening and went to buy us something to eat for the trip home. I was so angry that I did not want to talk to her.

We made the trip back to Kentucky without talking except once or twice. She spoke in an angry growl. I did not think about the fish in the live well until we were about two hours into our trip. At that point, I kind of smiled to myself and thought, "Oh, well. What was not my intention turned into a deceitful plan." I reasoned, "What Lauren does not know will not hurt her."

I had figured out what to do by the time we pulled into the gravel driveway by the sheds. She went to the toilet, and I went to the live wells. I pushed up the lids of each and lipped one big bass per hand. I ran down the hill to the top where my spring came out. The bass were in perfect shape, and I released them instantly without even having to revive them. The aerators had kept them lively and fresh, along with the Keep Alive that had already been in there.

I was back in the boat, flipping down the live well lids when Lauren came back out to the truck.

"What are you doing with the live wells?

"I don't know. I thought you had some plants in there or something."

"No, they're all in the bags." She tossed them out from the back of the truck.

"You're gonna talk to me now?" I asked.

"As long as you start listening to me like you are supposed to."

"Okay. From now on," I promised. "As long as you help me with those chub suckers and trout before you leave."

Lauren was not in the mood, but she gave me some quick lessons on my chub suckers and looked over my trout.

"These are ready," she said. "Too much bigger and you are going to spend your money raising big trout—not big bass."

"They're only five and half inches."

"Some may be six. That's a big trout for a three-pound bass."

"Ahh, maybe not," I said. I was thinking of Elise down in the depths now. She would swallow a couple six-inch trout without hesitation.

"Whatever. The chub suckers are not going to grow so fast. You can wait some more months on them. Throw in these spawners. You can continue to use the shallow end of the lake as your breeding area for these bigger ones. Once these others mature, you can use some of them to start the cycle all over. You can always net up some breeders too another time. Those would be easy to net up in those shallow corners."

She headed for the truck and gave me a kiss goodbye. She was surprised that I wanted to stay here. She made fun of my makeshift residence, but this was home for me now. I did not feel like moving to Belleville, and the few things I had in my trailer were now here in hog sheds, my fisheries sanctuary.

I figured the big bass I shocked up would not attend my dusk-time feedings tonight, but in the back of my mind, that is what I was looking for when I carried a bucket of rainbow trout toward the feeders.

The feeders came on as timed. The bluegill showed up, then a few redear, then some bass in the three-pound range. I saw one bigger bass over four pounds. I threw out about half the rainbows but did not see any being attacked. I saw them scurry away, with one confused, coming back to the surface in dangerous territory. A big bass from the bottom nailed it in one fast attack. More bluegill disappeared too. I dumped the rest of the bucket of rainbow at the spring and walked back to my shed for the night.

Chapter 10

A Fishy Dreamlike State

The days rolled into weeks. I spent my life feeding fish and rewriting my thesis. I had to send it back to my director several times before he finally approved it. I lived, breathed, and ate fish. I started eating two-pound bass as my main diet. They had successfully spawned and juvenile bass swam by everywhere, pegged by shadows beneath. I had not seen Elise, but I knew she was there with her younger sister, lurking in the depths, probably in one of my giant tree piles out in the middle. They were in their preferred zone, like home, with shad and bluegill to feed on, and plenty of deep cover. I hoped that as the summer warmed up, they might head toward my spring, under my giant pool cover, strapped down to four trees and shading 50 meters of my top-end channel. The water was deep there and at least eight degrees cooler than the surface temperature of the sunny areas.

I unfastened the 25-horsepower Johnson from my Alumacraft boat and dragged the empty boat down the hillside one wet, rainy day. I hauled the battery down later and connected it to the trolling motor and fish finder. I was going to find those beauties.

I trolled back and forth over the giant piles of trees in some of the deeper parts of the lake, looking like a maze of branches and sticks on the fish finder. Sure, you could see a suspended fish here and there, but these bleeps were not 12 or 17-pound bleeps. They were a few three-or-four-pound bass ranging for shad.

The next day, the Pond Boss guy, Bill, showed up to spray the lake. He had his aluminum boat ready as always.

"Hey, glad to see you," I said. "I put a boat down there now so you can use that from now on."

"That will make it easier," Bill said. "I'm also going to put in the aerator today. You want to show me where you want it?"

I showed Bill where I thought he should install the aerator. I wanted it closest to that nearby pond so none the muck from it infested my lake. I also did not want it too close to where I had planted my grasses from Lake Fork.

After he finished the installation and sprayed the lake, he told me the fisheries guy would be out later next week with the threadfin and some more bluegill. I was pleased about this.

Bluegill would still need to be replenished, since they were the best breeders. They were also much cheaper than the redear. The shad would thrive now that the lake had been fertilized. I would be installing more feeders in preparation for the bluegill. I was going to have them all around the lake now.

Toward the end of summer, the weather warmed, making it uncomfortable in my hog shed, even with a window AC unit I installed. I insulated the windows and doors where I could, but the hot summer was unrelenting. I did all I could to ensure my hatchery fish, especially the trout, stayed cool enough, but I had more die than normal that week. I decided to start dumping them in the lake by the pool cover, where they could live in the cool, shaded water, significantly colder than the runway. I installed another pellet feeder there and started dumping in trout every day at dusk.

I did this for about three days. I did not see any bass come up. I think they were feeding on the shad that were in huge abundance in the main lake area. However, the fourth day proved to be different. The pellets went in, followed by a flurry of bluegill activity, then some four-pound class bass. They were fat. I tossed in a couple trout. Pound! They were pegged right away. They were such an easy meal for the four-pound bass. I tossed in more. Bass ate them before they could swim a few meters. I had on my polarized glasses from earlier, and below this zone of activity, I could see one big shadow. I tossed in three or four more trout. Two of them became food right away, but two sped downward to the deeper spots. That's when I saw the 12-pound Lake Fork fish, which appeared to be 13 or 14 pounds already. She moved about three feet, and one of the bigger trout, about six inches, disappeared. She came in and scored another before dark.

I could not wait to wake up before daylight. I typically did not feed the bass any trout in the morning, but usually saved that for the evening. My hunch was that maybe I could entice Elise's sister to come up in the morning at the same feeder or maybe the opposite one. I tried the opposite one. I sat there waiting with two big five-gallon buckets of trout. Some of them were big ones too.

The feeder went off and the bluegill went nuts. Bass started eating too, and bluegill disappeared. I did not see the 13- or-14 pounder right away, but as the sun rose a little more, I was then able to see the giant down there in 10 feet of water, in the cool spot from the spring. I dumped in both buckets and watched.

Some of the smaller trout were eaten right away by the four-and-a-half-to-five-pound bass. Some of them sped down to deeper water, where I was hoping my big fish would eat a few quick meals. I saw her scoot up closer, stealthily and quietly, like a huge tank. She waited until a dumb trout swam right in front of her, and she inhaled it like air through her gills. A few minutes later, down deeper, I could make out the same thing in the shadows. A trout was swimming by, then a big suck in from the bass, and no more trout. One big swallow, and a six-inch trout disappeared whole.

My summer revolved around these feedings. I soon fed this bass all my trout except for a handful that I had reserved for breeding. I needed more.

I called all the fish hatcheries I knew about before finding a new hatchery in Tennessee that would stock the trout, after I told them my surface water temperature under the cover was right at 70 degrees, and it would be much cooler in the deeper spots where the spring came in. One of the hatchery guys warned me about the Largemouth Bass Virus, cropping up in the south and killing off many of the bigger bass. Lake Fork was one of the worst hit lakes. I had a pang of regret when he told me that, but the virus was not affecting my fish so far, so I did not worry. I negotiated a deal on the trout, and they loaded them up. I also ordered another shipment for October. After seeing the tremendous results with the fertilizer spraying, I called Bill to order additional sprayings. I wanted my threadfin to continue to grow big and repopulate.

"All I care about is results," I told him. I negotiated a long-term contract, but I had to put it on my credit card. I was out of cash.

After spending several thousand dollars on fish and fertilizer on the card, I was glad that I would be starting work soon. I couldn't keep this up forever. I would not tell Lauren about my spending spree; she had already harshly criticized me when she found out about the first spraying.

My life was like a dream that bass fishermen everywhere had, but even I could not stomach eating any more bass for a while. They were all over five pounds now, with fingerling bass pounded as food. I would have to start buying my meat elsewhere.

I heard some kids in the woods nearby playing close to the neighboring farm. The next day, I put out "NO TRESPASSING" signs all along the perimeter of my property, even though it bordered a farm on three sides, and was quite a ways from any road or place where people would ever see it. Nonetheless, I did not want anyone to find it now.

I had never weighed the biggest bass from Lake Fork, but I knew she had to be around 20 pounds by now. I could see the wide shape of her body in the depths. She was bigger than any bass anywhere.

I went to sleep that night, hot and sweaty from working outside, and thinking of my record bass, a Kentucky state record. I thought to myself, "Who are you kidding? That is a super bass from Texas. It is not even a northern bass. How could that be the Kentucky state record? What would Lauren say if she knew about this? Why didn't I tell her? I was mad, that's one reason. I hadn't planned it, two. It just happened."

I saw Lauren, her strawberry blonde hair up, curly and perfect. She was in a white dress, with a flowing gown on a hillside overlooking a trophy bass lake. I was dressed in a tuxedo, holding her hand and kissing her.

Then I saw this wonderful log house on a lake, overlooking bass on a quiet cove, as they swam by. The beautiful oak trees shaded the house and kept it cool on the warm spring day. Two babies ran around. One was 26 months; she was big, daddy's pride and joy, golden curls and giggles. The other was a little guy, 14 months old, running around with little legs holding daddy's fishy pole.

I awoke to the smell of fish and the bubbling and gurgling sounds of my aerators. Still in a dream state, I walked to the runways. Trout were floating in one. I was a bit disgusted. Luckily, I had released most of them a few weeks ago. My other raceways looked clean, so I just flushed the one. The trout would be food for the crayfish back in the shallow mud holes.

The chub suckers looked healthy and had grown to a decent size for their age. I decided I would release at least half of them today in the spring water. I arrived mid-feeding and dropped in about a hundred five-inch chub suckers. I did not wait to see what lurked below. I took another hundred and spread them out in the shallower areas of the lake, where they would live, grow, breed, and make this the greatest fishery that ever existed.

Chapter 11

End of the Summer Dream

I knew the summer was over when one day I was walking back toward my hill from putting out the rest of the chub suckers. I had decided to shut down my hatchery for a while. I had to attend training at Southwestern Illinois College in Belleville.

I noticed a mass floating on the shoreline on a shallow corner. When I walked closer to look, I almost threw up seeing the bloated bass. Not a five-pound bass, but maybe a 15-pound bass. My mind jumped back to what I had heard about the Largemouth Bass Virus at Lake Fork, and I thought the worst: my lake would be ruined with fish kill.

As I walked closer, I saw what had happened. In the bass' mouth was at least a two-and-a-half-pound bass—maybe bigger—stuck headfirst in the big bass' mouth. I couldn't believe it. "You dumb fish!" I yelled. "What were you thinking eating another bass? You have all the trout, shad, and suckers in the world!" The fish was clearly my smaller Lake Fork bass.

I found myself feeling distraught over the stupid fish. Why? I put so much into this fishery; I put my whole life into this. What had I gained from all my toils? What was it? A big crapshoot that could end with one fish becoming too greedy. Or just a fluke. The bass probably had eaten scrawny two-pound Lake Fork bass in past years. It could not swallow a bass of that same length with the girth of these fish, which were busting at the gut, full of shad and other food.

I loaded up my stuff and left for the day. I had not talked to Lauren in at least a month and did not have a phone here. I needed to find her and talk to her.

I felt somewhat ashamed that I had not ever visited Lauren at her apartment in St. Louis. I had talked to her a few times, and she was extremely busy with the new aquarium. She had shared that she worked all day to the point of exhaustion. She hated her job, but then again, this was the difficult ramp-up time.

I found her apartment and knocked on the door.

A small older woman with short blonde hair came to the door.

"Is this where Lauren lives?"

"Yes, I'm Lauren's mom. Are you Jay?"

"Yeah. So nice to meet you," I said, giving her a hug. She was a teacher and a farmer's wife. It was not my fault that we had never met. She lived hours away in northern Missouri and was busier than I was. "Where's Lauren?"

"She's here. I'm afraid there's been an accident, and Lauren broke her shoulder."

"No way," I said, concerned.

Lauren's mom led me to her dark room where Lauren was in a fog.

"Mom? Mom? Who is it?"

"Jay, that fishing nut you are always talking about."

Lauren's mom turned on the light. Lauren started to bawl, and I reached down to hug her gently as her arm was in a sling. Between sobs, she started to talk quickly. "That stupid guy had me lifting boulders into the tank, and not enough ladders or the right equipment," she sobbed. She started crying more and more without being able to continue as I held her.

Lauren's mom explained, "This girl thought a folding chair might do the job for lifting a boulder into a fish tank. Well, she was wrong."

Lauren cried for a while, still in a fog from her medication and the pain of having broken her shoulder.

I tried to say the right things, but I was a dunce, out feeding fish and stuff like that. Never calling or anything. I felt horrible.

Lauren went back to sleep, and I talked with her mom for a while, who had left the farm to come and take care of Lauren. She was the only person that would. Lauren had no way to call me. Lauren's mom had to return to the farm right away, and on top of that, school would start in a couple days as well for her.

I felt like a creep.

I said, "The least I could do is stay here and take care of her. I have to start some training on Monday and start teaching classes, but I only work about four hours at night, from 6:00 to 10:00 p.m., Mondays through Thursdays."

The next day we told Lauren the plan, and I had never seen her so happy. She smiled and tears came down her face. She was as broken as could be. In the days ahead, I would learn that she was giving up on her fisheries project and thesis. On top of that, she could not work. She was on worker's comp and that would last some weeks, but Lauren told me, "I'm never going back there. That is the most horrible place to work. In fact, I'm never going back into fisheries work—ever."

Again, the days turned into weeks, and the weeks into months. Lauren and I were closer than ever, and this misfortune had brought us to a place of strong commitment to each other. It made me realize that Lauren needed me, and maybe I needed her too. She recovered and found work at a lab at Monsanto. I started working for some software developers as a technical writer, in addition to teaching nights for Southwestern Illinois College.

The following May, I found myself on that hillside in my tuxedo as in my dream, standing above a bass lake on her aunt and uncle's property in Missouri. Our wedding was beautiful, and it was not a dream. As I stood there on the hillside looking down to the bass lake, I wondered how my bass lake was doing. Were my utilities even still on? Was my aerator working? Were my chub suckers thriving in the lake? Did the hatchery guy from Tennessee put in the small trout in October as I had told him? Was the heater sensor working? As I said, "in sickness and in health, 'til death do us part," I saw my world-record bass, Elise, and became confused. How could I be saying this? I have a world-record bass to catch. The thought went away in the flurry of activity following the wedding, honeymoon, and months later, finding our dream house on Lake Tishomingo, the log house in my dream.

One evening I was supposed to be teaching a class in Red Bud, Illinois. I left work hours early and headed a bit further south instead to my Kentucky honey hole.

The evening was mystical. Early fall was a perfect time for bass fishing. I called and canceled my class. I was going fishing in Kentucky instead. The drive took three hours speeding all the way.

I was surprised to see the aerator spraying up water as I looked down at the lake. It had been a long time since I had seen an electric bill. I must have paid ahead some the last time. I was relieved, knowing maybe my feeders were working too.

Nope. I saw that the first feeder was empty. I went to the shed and gathered food to refill it. I worked hard refilling the feeding stations all around the lake. Then, I took out my favorite fishing pole. This is the day I have been waiting for, I told myself.

As I started putting together my two-piece rod and tying on a crankbait, I thought to myself, "This fish still has so much food. Why would he bite this little crankbait?"

Nonetheless, I started fishing shallow with it. After about six casts, I hooked a huge fish. It fought so hard, I had to loosen my drag and let it play out. I was lucky to land it, as it missed tree limbs and wrapped up in some reeds at the shore. I lipped its jaw, opposite of where the treble hooks penetrated the fatty tissue of its mouth. This was now the fattest bass I have ever seen. It was shy of 10 pounds, but your average guy would have called it 10. Why not? Nine pounds, 10 ounces? That makes 10 in any fisherman's story, at least! My heart beat quickly. I fished some more and hooked another, only to lose it after it jumped. It too was big.

I hooked another right away, a small two pounder. "Oh crap," I thought to myself. "Some of those fingerlings have grown up already and are competing for food!" I kept it. No need to have over-competition keeping the big ones from growing.

The sky dimmed. The odds were that the big one still lurked deep in the shadows under the cover. That is probably where most of the surviving trout lived too.

I stood by the feeder and only waited about 10 minutes before it started spreading out the pellets. Bluegill came, then 10-pound bass, then a few smaller bass, but I stood there stunned at the big bass swarm. I mean, how often do you see a school of 10-pound bass? On top of that, how often do you see them pounding fish at your feet?

I couldn't help it. I made a short cast and pulled my brown-colored crank bait through the churning water. One bass spotted it and followed it for a bit, curious, then I paused it and started to retrieve it again, then bam!

A couple of short runs in the deeper water, and I held the fish in my hand. If I had to guess its weight honestly, I would say 10 pounds, 10 ounces. This fish was huge! As I held it and went to release it, I saw the shadow of Elise below. When my released fish swam to the bottom, it stirred up the big one to come up some more stealthily. I saw her suck up a big bluegill, and then a nine-inch rainbow trout was gone in a flash. I dropped my bait out like five feet in front of me because my heart was beating so fast that I could not cast or even consider what would be the best presentation.

I saw the giant female come back around, and I could scan over her whole length and girth. I knew then that I was looking at a world-record bass, easily weighing 24 pounds, if not 26 pounds, at least two pounds bigger than George Perry's 22-pound-four-ounce record from 1933 in Georgia.

My crankbait floated untouched on the top of the water as the feeder continued to spread out pellets. Most of the bluegill had disappeared, probably either eaten or scared to death. A few trout were still swimming around eating the pellets, like idiots. A 10-pound bass nailed another trout. I reeled in my crankbait, and the fish ignored it. Too much food right here that looks better.

The sun went down, but the water churned some more in this spot and others where I had refilled the feeders. I had to return home with a long drive ahead of me.

Later that night about 10:50 p.m., Lauren asked me about my class and told me about her day. I was in another realm and so happy. I held her and kissed her and loved her like my days were filled with her and fishing. Forget tech writing, home inspections, and the new home. This was all a dream. My real world was at my lake.

By this point, I couldn't stop thinking about my record bass, but I had a honey-do list a mile long, a new house needing work, and a pregnant, unhappy wife. That didn't include three jobs: one in software development, one college, and an online university. I did not have time to fish, much less catch the world record.

About this time, I heard about the guys who fish Dixon Lake in San Diego. My mom asked me if I had heard the story. She lived in California and asked me if I had heard the news. I looked it up online, read all about it, and followed the story for a few months. It made me think about my fishery and all the questions that came with it.

Mac Weasley put in the time and dedication to locate and hook the world-record bass in Lake Dixon, close to San Diego. He hooked a 25-pound-one-ounce bass, but he unintentionally foul hooked the fish through the dorsal fin. It probably was trying to brush the jig away from its bed and that is why Mac felt it and set the hook into it. The catch would not hold up to the scrutiny of the International Game Fish Association (IGFA).

The more and more I thought about this, the worse I felt. Mac and his friends did the right thing in releasing the fish and not trying to claim a world record. Could I do that? If I caught my record bass, I could not say it was a Kentucky bass. Lauren would not tolerate that. She would know better. How could I have raised it when all my other fish were under 11 pounds? No one would believe me. Not only that, but how would I explain this to Lauren?

Another Mac came to mind...they called him Big Mac, St. Louis Cardinals' own, Mark McGwire. He broke the world record for the most home runs in a season in 1998 with 70 home runs. He was our local hero with his picture on the front page of the newspaper. The city of St. Louis even renamed the highway after him. In 2005, Congress subpoenaed him, and he skirted around answering questions about his and others' use of illegal steroids as performance-enhancing drugs, raising all kinds of ethical questions about various records in the books. They all need to have asterisks under them. That would be true about the bass in my lake too, if I were ever able to catch it. My whole life's work was one big asterisk.

The more I thought about the issue, the more I realized that the truth would come out if I ever lied about this. Instead, I decided to pursue my bass, but make it something of legends and myths, like the mythology class I was teaching online, and never claim it as a record. It would be a fantasy or a thing of fiction, like my discussions online about Bigfoot.

More time went by. I studied and purchased some new equipment I planned to use at the lake. I ordered more stocker trout. I purchased all of it on a credit card Lauren did not know about. I asked her once for a deal that if I let her have a baby, she would let me buy more trout for my lake. She acted as if that were just a joke, but I told her it wasn't. She did not talk to me for a few days after that, and I learned that if I had something I needed to do for my lake, I had better keep it to myself.

Chapter 12

A New World-Record* Bass

I was at our Missouri lake with my newborn baby and Lauren at home full time. I had more responsibilities than ever, but I had to take a few days off to visit my Kentucky lake. Lauren had agreed to this. I arrived in Kentucky Friday night after dark and spent the evening spooling up line and prepping gear. I had two rods set up. Stout rods that could handle a 27-pound bass. I also used 15-pound test green P Line that I soaked in hot water first. I tied on a Castaic rainbow trout lure, the seven-inch model. I also tied on a soft plastic Castaic shad lure that actually looked like a rather odd shad, more like one of my chub suckers in color and size.

The next morning, I was up before dawn; the weather was cool. To me, it felt perfect at 60 degrees Fahrenheit. I was keeping my honey hole close to this temperature almost year round. I knew that contributed to the conditions that allowed this fish to grow to world-record size.

I started with the Castaic trout lure. It looked so soft and real. I started away from my spring and figured I would return there later when the feeders went off. I cast out as far as I could with my new rod and reel. A smooth perfect cast went far out into deep water. I let it sink for about 10 seconds and began a slow, slow retrieve, barely enough to keep that trout tail thumping.

The sun started to come over the horizon. As I reeled slowly, I marveled at the lake I had created. The vegetation was in full bloom, with hyacinths, bull rushes, water willow, piles of Christmas trees in various places in about eight feet of water, deadfalls, and several different kinds of grasses. My bass lake was surely the greatest ever built. On top of that, here I was fishing with a seven-inch trout lure for fish over 10 pounds. Maybe even the world record.

I felt a fast peg and reeled hard, but nothing. One had hit and missed. I slowed down my retrieve. The bait was not swimming perfectly, I thought, and came to the top too fast. I had difficulty keeping it in the deep areas. I decided to try the Castaic shad bait instead with the little bill. That seemed to swim more naturally than the other bait. I let it sink for about 10 seconds and retrieved it in a tight wobble, slowly. Half way back, BAM! Hookup!

The fish was tearing out drag. I had to tighten it and set the hook again. Luckily, I did that fast enough to keep it hooked. The fish tried to jump, and I steered it back by angling my rod to the side and down. It made a couple of runs and tried to go for a big snag of tree limbs. I reeled it in hard, away from the snag to the shoreline. The fish gave up for a few seconds, enough for me to lip it. The fish was the biggest I had ever caught. I pulled out my new Islamorada BogaGrip. It pulled it all the way down to the 12 line. I'd call it 12 pounds even. Fat fish! Healthy! Incredible girth! I threw it back.

I was shaking from the excitement, and I walked to my favorite feeder by the spring. I stood there and waited. I saw a little billowing under the pool cover to my left, probably bubbles from the big rains we had, coming in from the spring in gushes of air pockets, or maybe something else, something bigger was causing the billows.

When the pellets from the feeder started going out, trout came up right away, even before the bluegill. I pitched out my lure and let it sink down to the bottom. It did not look natural as it sank since it was not swimming, but the color and shape looked realistic. I then reeled it in like an injured chub sucker trying to escape. As I had hoped, I saw the shadow of my giant move closer to inspect it. Nothing that cast, but the big girl was waiting for a trout to make a dumb move or for an injured chub sucker or bluegill to fall down toward her.

Big bass started pegging the bluegill and trout. I counted at least 12. I did not see any small bass here. They would have been bait too. Every fish was at least 10 pounds or better. I saw Elise gulp in a trout down below. She was patient and waited. She did not school like the others, who had been raised on a fish farm in their early lives.

I pitched my soft plastic bait back down to the big bass and watched her reaction. She was watching and turned. I twitched it and made it swim a bit. She grabbed it. I reeled up line and went to set the hook, but she spit the lure out of her mouth. The bait shot about eight feet up the water column with my ridiculous, nervous hook set.

I did not have the experience or fortitude for a fish like this, especially with 15-pound test line and a couple small treble hooks. I realized the only way I was going to hook this big fish was with a big jig and some pork. I went back to the shed and spooled up 20-pound-test P Line. I tied on a huge jig with a big 6/0 Gamakatsu hook and a big piece of brown pork. The jig was green and brown. I quickly changed the timers on the feeders so they would go off again in a few minutes.

I went inside for a bite to eat and came back. The feeders turned on again. I looked down and could not see Elise down there, but I knew she would be. I tossed my jig to the opposite shoreline in front of my cover. I let the jig sink slowly to the bottom. Then I bounced it along. Right in the middle, I knew she was there, and I felt the fish engulf my jig, even though I could not see her. I set the hook immediately without giving her a chance to spit. She was hooked, one solid rock of a fish like the one I hooked on Lake Fork, which had been wedged behind a stump. She started moving to deeper water in the main lake, and I turned my drag down a notch to let her have a run. She did a couple of short ones and ran out of steam. I started pumping her in. When I pulled her close, she did not make any effort to run again, like most green fish. She was lazy. I lipped her with one hand, set my rod down, and grabbed the back of her body at the tail. This fish was too huge to hold up with one hand.

I marveled at how fat she was. She had eaten trout after trout and sucker after sucker, I imagined. Maybe even some bass. I knew she had eaten many bluegill. I had seen her. She probably ate any shad that veered back here in the winter, unknowing. She might have even swum out and nailed frogs, crayfish, and other fish. I was one proud papa. The sad feeling came over me then that this was not my baby. She was a Lake Fork beauty, which could not be claimed as the world record.

With my BogaGrip in my pocket, I had to weigh her, even if it might be a bit hard on her. I clasped her jaw with the grip right at the lower front where the bone was strong and gently released her head and tail so the scale could weigh her accurately. It went a hair past the line between 26 and 28. Elise was over 27 pounds.

I passed on the temptation to put her in one of my runways. I knew that could potentially kill her. By God, she might not live that much longer anyway. I saw myself in the same position as Mac Weasley. I knew this moment would come. I put her back and held her tail and lower jaw to let her revive for a few seconds until I saw her gills moving open and shut. I released her. She swam slowly down to the bottom of my top pool there under the cover into the shadows. Clearly, that was her favorite haunt, except when she came out to eat or sun herself.

I basked in the moment and walked the shoreline of my lake. I bailed out the boat and pushed off to enjoy the late morning with my rods in hand. Heck, I might even fish some more. Why not?

The sun was up now, and the fall day warmed quickly. I decided to try my rainbow trout lure back in some shallower areas. How would the big bass respond to it?

I fished different retrieves without much luck and just one miss. I returned to the soft plastic shad bait and had more success. The first hookup came in about five feet of water and was a spectacular explosion right off the bat as the fish came out of the water after my hook set. I lifted the fish in the boat and weighed it. Over 11. The sun was overhead now, and the bites subsided. I headed in.

Chapter 13

Back to Reality

After a fishing trip like this, going back to work the following Monday was brutal. It made the fishing experience seem like a fantasy, a dream, and I wasn't sure it truly happened. Did I really catch the world-record bass? I hooked it, right in the jaw, fair and square. I knew I could not tell about it—not even Lauren should know about this. Some secrets were worth keeping. That's how I felt about it. I had created what was like the "Area 51" of Bass Fishing. The slogan for my fishery could be "THE WORLD-RECORD BASS IS OUT THERE."

I started thinking about my world-record fishery so much and was so exuberant about it, that I started writing about my experience on my laptop. When I had a chance, I wrote down my notes on my whole creation and my successes with my trout and chub suckers, and now my world record. This was the greatest bass fishing story ever told, maybe even more fanciful than Mac Weasley's tale or others I have heard.

The one thing I learned about marriage is that if you do something and lie about it or try to cover it up, your spouse will eventually find out. That's exactly what happened with Lauren. She knew I had been fishing, and she knew I had 10-pound bass in my lake. She knew I was exuberant about it. When she read my story off my laptop, everything changed. Lauren was angry, but I did not feel that I deserved to be the target of her rage. She was yelling so loudly that I could not even make sense of what she was saying. This is the gist of the conversation:

"What were you thinking? Stealing bass from Lake Fork with SIU's research boat, shocking fish and transplanting them to your lake. Like a 10-pound bass is not big enough? Your ego was not satisfied? You had to raise a 27-pound bass? You spent like

$100,000 on some remote lake that no one has ever fished except you for a few hours? For what, you selfish jerk? You could have gotten me into all kinds of trouble!"

"What?" I yelled back. "They would not have fired you over that. It's a university. You don't think any of your colleagues ever did anything like transplanting fish? I was trying to help you that night before you got so angry over me using the boat. I was going to help you tag and release the fish, but you were so mad that you wouldn't even talk to me!"

The arguments went on for months. Lauren stayed at home and raised our daughter. She had given up on working or finishing her thesis.

Life went on, and I was miserable, having created such a rift in my marriage because of my obsession with my lake. Those winter nights I imagined myself at the bottom of Lake Tishomingo, "accidentally" wrapped around my boat's anchor. My routine was oppressive, working at the office in communications and at college. I was teaching as many as nine classes online at a time while working full time with a two-hour commute round trip. After 11 hours away from home working, I returned home to do my online teaching and grading for several hours. I spent my weekends grading papers and dealing with students. On top of that, I did dishes, cleaned up messes, and completed all the home repairs and improvements. I worked so hard that I did not even fish in our back yard on the lake where we lived. Somehow, after all my hard work, I still had not regained Lauren's trust. We decided to have another baby—maybe that would help. She promised that everything would be better if we did. Less than a week later, she was showing me the positive pregnancy test, ecstatic. I was happy about the news too.

Marriage and family are full of issues that I could never figure out, no matter how hard I tried. How was it that I married a fisheries biologist who hates fish and detests fishing? Lauren swore that she would never finish that Master's thesis and was sick of it. I did not know how to help her or how to make it right. I went to counseling alone and talked out the problems for months simply so I could sleep at night.

Missouri experienced the wettest spring in its recorded history. It rained and rained and rained. Lauren and I had had a big fight, and we hadn't been talking. She had accused me of being insensitive and being more concerned about my fish than about her. She was probably right, but I did not know how to change. She told me she could never trust me again. She withdrew into her room and into watching TV, and we did not have much of a relationship at all. In the heat of one argument, she said that she hoped my lake's earthen dam would break and that all those fish would die. That I deserved it because I put all that time and money into that useless lake. Her family farm levy broke in 1993 and some years later as well, and they lost everything those years. I did not understand why she hated my fishery so much and wanted my dream to come to ruin.

The rain slowed Friday afternoon, and I decided to drive to Kentucky and fish my lake. I pulled in the gravel driveway and unloaded my tackle. I tied on my favorite soft plastic bait and headed down to the hill. Some daylight remained, and a foggy mist filled the air.

I came down the hill and saw the worst sight I have ever seen. My pool cover that I would normally see first was gone, as was all the water in that top spring cove. Water was coming out of the spring as a frothy, bubbling river. It made a huge swirling mud hole below like the Mississippi River looked earlier when I crossed it.

I walked down the hill all the way, and the damage was even worse. The lake was half-empty, and the lower side dam was blown, where the creek, now a gurgling river, exited. I fell to my knees and clenched my head in my hands. I felt broken from this and from the horrible things I had been through with Lauren. "It's all a waste," I thought to myself.

I cried, thinking about how my lake was ruined. It hurt the most knowing that the world-record bass might be gone too. She could be down that river. I surveyed the damage, and it was a mess—one big mud hole.

I looked out in the middle by my tree piles. There might be more than five feet of muddy water out there, I figured. There would still be some bass there. Even the marshy end probably had plenty of chub suckers and bluegill on that flooded plain, even all the way to the crappy frog pond. Even so, it was a huge loss, maybe something from which the lake would never recover.

In my mind's eyes, I envisioned Lauren behind the controls of a big earthmover, as if she were at her dad's farm. She approached my earthen dam from the back where the spring overflow came out. Her hair was bright red instead of her usual strawberry blonde, and she had an angry look on her face. She had the engine going full steam ahead and lowered the big front-end loader, plowing straight into the dam. The dam blew with an explosion of water and mud into the air, but she continued forward until the whole lake drained. A three-and-a-half-foot stream of water engulfed her machine, stuck there. She was laughing and happy though. "To hell with this fishery. I am glad the dam blew!"

Her wishes came true in my open vision as I stood there, bewildered at the sight of this mess. The sun came and started to burn off the fog. I trudged through the mud and walked down the shoreline toward the middle of the lake, where I still had at least 20 acres of a lake in the middle of what once was 70 acres. I probably had another 30 acres of shallow flooded marsh down at the far end. I knew that any bass would probably be in this deeper spot though. I started sinking deeper until I had lost my shoes in the mud, and I was still 15 feet from the water line. I did not care. I was tenacious now. I made my first cast with my muddy rod and reel and my shad lure at the end. My cast made it, and I started swimming the shad slowly under the surface. BAM! Four seconds into my retrieve, I hooked a huge bass. It flopped around like crazy in all directions, without a place to dive down for a run. It broke off, and I dragged my bait through the mud back to me.

I painstakingly cleaned off the bait onto my shirt. After several minutes of that, I cast out again until I hooked another bass. Another big one hit. The fish made wild jumps and flops in the now shallower water. I reeled it to the shoreline and dragged it up a few feet into the mud. It flopped around like crazy again after a short rest, then covered in mud, it broke the line and flopped back in. I was relieved to see some 12-to-14-pound bass in the lake, maybe some bigger ones remained.

I surveyed the dam and all the damage. Water still flowed like a fast stream from the spring. The greatest attribute of this lake, the underground spring, became its undoing. I figured that it would take some serious dry weather, then an engineering contractor to build a professionally-designed dam. I cringed, thinking about what it could cost: $30 to $40,000? I could only guess.

In the meantime, I bought some huge pieces of plywood at the local hardware store and created three walkways down to the lake holes. I put my feeders there and also hand fed the fish for some days. I also called two hatcheries and ordered golden shiners, threadfin, and bluegill on my credit card. Bass would eat them right away probably, but they had some flooded areas to hide too, I reasoned. I also ordered three aerators.

I fell asleep in my rickety cot that night, tearful and sad. I sought answers to the questions that this messy life brings. My mind raced around. I thought of one episode I saw on *Bassmaster* a few years earlier. A reporter interviewed a guy and his wife about chasing the bass fishing tournament dream. They had sold their house and were going to use the money to live on the B.A.S.S. trail. The interview was positive and they were excited, but the emptiness of their decision was apparent. Of course, *Bassmaster* never provided a follow-up story on the couple's pursuit. In fact, isn't it odd that you never hear stories on the hundreds of tournament anglers that failed and went bankrupt, without any wins to their names and no money in their bank accounts? I thought about people like these and about some of the local guides I had fished with in Florida and other places. Their lives were often similar. Big dreams, but the complexities of life never allowed them to actualize them. Some of them lived in trailers similar to mine by the Refuge, and some lived in their trucks. I thought of the guy in Mississippi who tried to raise the world-record bass. A few of his fish reached 11 pounds, but his algorithm was much worse than mine, and his numbers of fish went sky high while his food supply plummeted. He was one of the many whose wives gave up on him. I racked my brain to think of people who had made it big. I could only think of a few and even they had problems and made sacrifices. Everybody admires Kevin VanDam and his successes on the water. If they only knew how much time and work he put in on the water too. Most of these men with huge tournament successes have never caught records either. I thought of Shaw Grigsby, who had some wins to his name, but in one tournament, he had to disqualify himself over some dumb rule that only he remembered for asking a fan about how his fishing went that day. He wasn't looking for any secrets or tips, but was merely being friendly.

Last, as I started to fade off to sleep, I forgot about all those American dreamers and thought about an article I had read last month. Japanese bass fisherman, Manabu Kurita, religiously fished his local waters in Lake Biwa, Japan. For many years, he pursued the giant largemouth bass that grew there because he loved it, despite the disdain Japanese officials and commercial fishermen had for the largemouth bass as an invasive junk fish. Manabu pursued his dream and landed a 22-pound, five-ounce world-record bass. The International Game Fish Association recognized the fish as a tie with George Perry's 22-pound, four-ounce record. A new record must be over two ounces to break the old record. After the IGFA certified the record, IGFA conservation director Jason Schratwieser said, "It's the Holy Grail of freshwater fishing." My thoughts of admiration fixed on Manabu and his achievement, and the irony of this whole pursuit.

I found myself praying for wisdom in my pursuits and faded off into a dream, or was it a vision of what is to come?

Epilogue

I was somewhere in the future but not sure when. The

moment was real or at least as real as a dream can be. The sky

was a blue azure without any hint of wind. The grass was perfect

as if it had been rolled on by the best grass landscaper. The

lakeshore was manicured without any weeds on the shoreline,

without chiggers or bugs of any kind. Without even needing my

polarized glasses, I could see the bass in the clear water. They

hung in big schools, fish over 20 pounds, some even 25 to 26

pounds, fat fish suspended in the water column in perfect

temperatures of 68 degrees Fahrenheit.

I did not have a fishing pole with me. I might not even own

one; I wasn't sure. I also no longer had the desire to catch these beautiful fish. I did not have any lust for it. I admired them and

enjoyed watching them. I was one with the lake and the

landscape of the green grass. The lake did not have any tangles or

deadfalls. Somehow, it did not need them. The fish were perfectly

suited to their habitat and had everything they needed. The

algorithm of this fishery was truly perfect; was it mine or

someone else's? I did not know, but I enjoyed it and relished the

moment with languor. I would stay here as long as I could in my

dream, my reality.

About the Author

Jason Covington studied creative writing at Pepperdine University and later earned a Master's degree in literature from Southern Illinois University at Carbondale. There he wrote a Master's thesis on "Fishing in America: Hemingway, Maclean and Duncan," and is clearly influenced by the work of University of Chicago Professor Norman Maclean. A university instructor himself, Covington has taught writing at eight colleges and universities since 1993. Traveling and fishing all over America, he learned the love for bass fishing at an early age. He brings the sport to life with stories from his own life as well as the dreamlike narrative of his alter ego in his first novella on the subject.

About "American BeheMouth"

"American BeheMouth" is a timely literary work that
depicts American moral equivalencies and excesses. For
fishermen, baseball fans, book lovers, sports enthusiasts, and
economists alike, the novella is highly entertaining and insightful.

Based on true fisheries science and sports history,
"American BeheMouth" tells the greatest bass fishing story of all
time while giving an insight into what America has become. On
the surface, the story is about a literature student and his
fisheries biologist girlfriend who raise the world-record bigmouth
bass in a Kentucky lake. Underneath, the novella is much more
than a fishing story; it is a metaphor for many other things: life,
family, sacrifice, commitment, and dreams. In addition, it raises

ethical questions about modern American sports, American businesses and consumerism, and our quest for the elusive. "American BeheMouth" is a metaphor for many things that are wrong in American culture, including the relentless pursuit for more, mirroring and predicting the many bubbles in the American economy.

In the big picture, the author may be asking all the existential questions while writing about fishing. In all, everyone can glean something from the story with humor and inquisitiveness.

www.ingramcontent.com/pod-product-compliance
Lightning Source LLC
Chambersburg PA
CBHW070928130626
46555CB00001B/337